BRENDA DELAMAIN was born in England. She's been a nurse, a farmer, a student and the mother of three children. Her fascination with local history led to the research that produced *Lizzie, love*. She has lived in Kerikeri for thirty-five years.

Kemp House, Kerikeri.

Lizzie, love

BRENDA DELAMAIN

Longacre Press

Acknowledgements:
The author wishes to thank the many people who helped
her with research, information and suggestions, in particular
Bella Wynyard for her Maori translations.

ISBN 1 877361 39 9

First published by Longacre Press, 2006
30 Moray Place, Dunedin, New Zealand

A catalogue record for this book is available from
the National Library of New Zealand.

Cover and book design by Christine Buess
Cover background lithograph by Antoine Chazal and Louis François Lejeune/
Museum of New Zealand Te Papa Tongarewa (I.028415)
Book illustrations by Brenda Delamain
Printed by McPherson's Printing Group, Australia

Contents

For Charlotte

CHAPTER 1

Elizabeth opened her eyes. Loud voices from outside had woken her. That wasn't unusual, but the light through the window was grey, and much too pale for her usual waking hour. And who was the speaker? She lay still, listening. Not her father, nor one of the other missionaries. Not one of her brothers. Not a Maori. No, this was definitely English.

'Tie her up, lad.' It was a cheerful, ringing voice.

Strangers!

Immediately Elizabeth was wide awake. Pushing back the bedcovers she reached for the crutches that always stood by the bed, hoisted herself to her feet, and limped across to the window.

It was a misty morning; the haze clung low and dense over the waters of the Kerikeri inlet. To her right the block of the new stone store loomed through the mist, encased in its framework of scaffolding. In the opaque half light Elizabeth could see movement on the foreshore below. Some men were there, pulling up a rowing boat; it crunched on the pebbles.

Her first thought was to tell her father but when she opened her bedroom door, he was already descending the stairs. At the same time her older brother, Henry, came from his room, hastily stuffing his shirt into his breeches. Her father glanced up.

'You heard them too, Lizzie, did you? I think it's Captain Dean off *The Elizabeth*. I know that voice. Come on then, lad, we'll go and see them.'

Elizabeth watched her father and brother patter down the stairs in their bare feet, and returned to the window just in time to see them come out of the door below, lifting their feet awkwardly as they walked along the stony path. They went through the gate in the fence that surrounded the mission settlement and scrambled down to the rocky beach below.

'Hello there, James Kemp,' came the same bluff voice that had woken her a few minutes earlier. 'An early morning call to wake you up,' was followed by a bray of laughter.

Elizabeth heard the door of her parents' room open then shut, and the soft sound of her mother's feet descending the stairs. She wondered for a second whether to go back to bed, but quickly decided to get dressed and go down. After all she was up now so why miss out on anything that was going on?

A few minutes later she was limping down the stairs, clinging to the bannister with one hand and holding her crutches with the other. The front door was flung open and her father came in with Captain Dean. Two sailors and Henry followed.

Mr Kemp was talking as he ushered them in. 'No, no, you must have some breakfast. My wife will be up now and it won't take long to prepare. We can't let you go with nothing to eat on a chilly morning.' He caught sight of Elizabeth on the bottom step. 'Ah, Lizzie, you'll go tell your mother there'll be three more for breakfast, will you, love?'

The Captain suddenly smiled broadly. 'Elizabeth, yes, I remember you.'

'And I remember you. You are the captain of my ship, *The Elizabeth*. And how is my ship?' she asked in a commanding tone.

The Captain jumped to attention and saluted. 'Well now, Madam, I beg to report that we have had a good voyage. The ship is in good heart, as is the crew. Isn't that so, men?'

The two sailors snapped their hands to their foreheads with exaggerated smartness.

'Aye, aye, Sir,' they chorused.

Elizabeth giggled at this play-acting and hopped down the last step.

'But what is this I see?' said the Captain. 'Last time I was here you had two good pins; have you been falling and breaking something?'

There was a moment's silence. Elizabeth hated to hear talk of her misfortune, of the lifeless leg beneath her skirts. She regarded it like a small reluctant child that had been left with her to be cared for and which she resented. She looked at her father as though expecting him to reply but, as he did not, she answered sharply. 'No, I'm afraid this pin is rather useless. But it will come right.'

'Unfortunately,' her father went on, 'Elizabeth was ill last year with a high fever and pains in her limbs. It has left her with this paralysed leg. We do not know why, but we pray for her recovery — if it be the will of the Lord.'

Elizabeth, embarrassed, made abruptly for the kitchen. But, before she could escape, the door opened and her mother came out. Mrs Kemp held out her hand and smiled in welcome.

'Captain Dean. James thought it was your voice we heard. I hope you and your men are staying for breakfast?' Her expression of kindness and sincerity quickly overcame the impression of a short, dumpy, rather plain woman.

'Well, your husband has been kind enough to ask us.'

'Good, then come through into the kitchen while I get it ready. I couldn't bear to think of you talking out here and me missing all the news. It's warmer there, too.'

The kitchen was small and unlined with a big brick fireplace and oven taking up most of one wall. A table and chairs occupied the available floor space.

A young Maori woman was standing over the stove. She turned and smiled shyly as they entered.

'This is Mere Taua who helps me,' said Mrs Kemp.

The men nodded to her and Mere turned back to the stove. The Captain sat down and looked about him. He seemed to see Henry for the first time.

'Is this young James, then?' he asked.

'No, this is our eldest son, Henry. James is our second son.'

'Ah, yes, Henry,' said the Captain mysteriously. 'Now, I have a message regarding Henry.'

Henry was sitting by the stove, putting on his socks. He looked up, startled.

'Regarding Henry?' asked his mother.

'Yes, ma'am. You see, as I came down the coast, I called in at Whangaroa and there I spoke to Captain Sadler of *The Buffalo* and to a Reverend Yates who was up there. They were discussing passage back to England.'

'I see,' said Mr Kemp heavily. 'Is Mr Yates thinking of going on *The Buffalo*?'

'And he wants to take Henry with him,' said Mrs Kemp as she lifted a pot of soaked oats over to the stove. It was as though she knew it already.

'Well dear, we have discussed it with him,' said Mr Kemp quietly.

'Yes, but so soon!'

Mr Kemp explained to the Captain. 'You see, we have decided that it is best that Henry goes back to England for his future education. It is best,' he repeated to his wife, touching her hand.

'You mean that Henry is going back to England now?' said Elizabeth. 'Truly?' She could hardly imagine what it would be like without her big brother to confide in.

'And the two Edwards?' asked Henry.

'Aye, they did mention Edward Clarke and Edward Williams. Messages have gone to them, too.'

Henry turned to his parents. 'Am I really going?'

'Indeed you are,' said his mother, picking up a wooden spoon and stirring the oats. 'You'll see all your relatives at Wymondham. And go to school in Norwich with Edward Clarke. He's going there too. They are good friends of ours, the Clarkes.' She paused, and clasped the spoon in both hands. 'We have lots of good friends there. You'll be safe. And you are fourteen now.'

'When does Captain Sadler wish to depart?' Mr Kemp cut in.

'In three days,' said the Captain. 'I'm sorry to give you such short notice ma'am. He also asks if you would not mind the lad embarking at Whangaroa as he has to load up with spars there, and it would save him a day.'

'We'll be ready,' she said. 'Now what have you brought for us? Are there any letters?'

'Ah, and I nearly forgot.' The Captain patted his coat and then reached into the inner pocket to produce a packet of letters tied with tape, which he handed to Mrs Kemp.

She looked through them quickly, sorting them into heaps on the table. The worried frown disappeared from her face as she shuffled through them. 'These are for the Shepherds and the Edmonds. I'll send them over. Here's one for you, James, from the Reverend Tacy. And Candell Clarke too. Oh, and one from sister Anne. We'll read them later.' She put the letters together and levelled them with a sharp tap on the table.

Elizabeth, meanwhile, had moved to where she was able to lift the cutlery from the sideboard across to the table, while standing on one leg. She had developed a great sense of balance since her setback.

The Captain leant back in his chair and looked about the kitchen. 'I trust the rest of the family is well?'

'Yes, indeed, we are very lucky,' said Mr Kemp. 'Barring Elizabeth's trouble, all seven of our children are healthy, with another due in a few months' time. Considering our lack of medical help, we are remarkably fortunate.'

'It certainly seems a healthy place, not like some of the hotter climes we call at.'

'But what's the news in England; what's happening over there?' asked Mr Kemp.

'Well, 'tis several months since I left England, myself,' said the Captain, 'but, as far as I know, King William is still on the throne. As I recall, the act abolishing slavery in his Majesty's dominions was passed in parliament shortly before our departure. Not that I think that would affect you much here.'

While the men talked, Mrs Kemp continued to stir the porridge,while Elizabeth hopped around the table, laying out the cutlery. When she reached Henry, on an impulse, she put her arms around his neck, dropping the remaining spoons on the table. The clatter drew everyone's attention.

'I wish you didn't have to go,' she mumbled into his collar.

Henry detached himself, stiff with embarrassment before the visiting sailors. 'Come on, Lizzie, don't be silly.'

'But it's so far away, and for such a long time.'

'It's not that long. You'll see, it'll be gone in no time. Then I'll be back.'

'It is a long time,' insisted Elizabeth. 'Three years! Have you thought how long a year is? Three hundred and sixty-five days. That is nine hundred and … um … three times sixty-five … which is … um …'

Everyone laughed, including Elizabeth.

'Oh, Lizzie, trust you to complicate things,' said Henry. 'Get on with the table.'

But he had to bite his lip to stop tears springing to his eyes. 'I don't suppose things will ever be the same again, though. You might not even be here when I come back,' he said softly. Elizabeth, hopping around his chair, was the only one to hear him.

'We will still be the same though,' she whispered. 'And I don't think they will move us down south. They couldn't, could they?'

Their father was obviously discussing the same matter with the visitors: the proposal of the church committee to move them to a new station, at a place called Tauranga. 'I've written to the committee,' he stated. 'I've told them we will not even contemplate it, and neither should they. They even talk of abandoning this station. It's ridiculous! Leaving these buildings which have cost them so much. And imagine my wife and my family being exposed to all the trials and labours attendant upon the formation of a new station. It is a position for younger men. And what about the natives here, we can't just abandon them? They are our friends.'

Mr Kemp thumped the table with the flat of his hand. 'It is quite out of the question, and I have written and told them so. And so has George Clarke.'

Mrs Kemp came over to the table with a stack of porridge plates and spread them out ready to be filled.

CHAPTER 2

After breakfast Mr Kemp departed with the Captain and Mr Shepherd, the other missionary stationed at Kerikeri. Mr Edmonds, the stonemason from Australia who had been working on the store, went too. It was a heavy job, manhandling the mission cases from *The Elizabeth* onto *Te Karere*, the mission cutter. Henry was eager to follow, but as he rushed for the door, his mother laid a detaining hand on his arm.

'James can go to help. I want you here.'

'But Mother …'

'No, Henry, if you are to go in two days, you have a lot to do here.'

'What can I do here? I'd be more use helping with the cases.'

'And even more time away,' she said, with a trace of bitterness.

Henry paused, then said, 'Alright Mother, what do you want me to do?'

'Firstly, go to your room and sort your clothes. Bring down those that need washing and anything that might need mending. You will have to sort your school books too and see which you may need to take with you. I'll get John Taua to bring a trunk down from the attic.'

Elizabeth came through from the kitchen and she turned to her. 'Ah, Lizzie, now you could hem some handkerchiefs, couldn't you? I wonder if I have time to finish those new shirts? The girls can have their sewing class today and they can do handkerchiefs too. It's as well to have a good supply. I've been meaning to do these jobs for weeks. I should have been more prepared. Oh! and there's the washing. I'll have to tell Mere to get the copper started and John could split some more wood for her. Thomas Reo could carry up the water.' She stood at the foot of the stairs, counting things off on her fingers.

'It sounds as though you are organizing the army,' laughed Henry.

'Sometimes it feels like that, I assure you.' Suddenly their mother turned and called up the stairs, 'Mary Ann, are you getting dressed?'

Elizabeth's nine-year-old sister came out onto the landing and sat on the top step waving a stocking. She was almost a replica of her older sister; each had long, dark brown hair plaited into a single braid that hung down her back. They had both inherited their mother's small build, though Mary Ann was the shorter, being younger by three years. Elizabeth had her Mother's large dark eyes and well-curved eyebrows, whereas it was a constant source of disappointment to Mary Ann that she had taken after her father with his heavy brows. However, she consoled herself with the thought that she had a better shaped nose and smaller feet. To Elizabeth, appearance was a matter of complete indifference.

'I'm up,' said Mary Ann 'but I couldn't find my other

stocking. I expect Lizzie has taken it because she hasn't darned hers. She thinks I don't know.'

'What an awful thing to say; it's not true, Mama,' said Elizabeth hotly. 'Hers would be far too small, anyway.'

'Oh, Mary Ann, fancy accusing your sister. I'm sure if anyone is behind in their darning, it is more likely to be you. However, we'll sort that out later. Please go and see that Richard is getting up and then help William and Sarah to wash and dress.'

'But, Mama, William won't do as I say.'

'Well, tell him he must or he'll answer to me. Now be a help, dearest. I'll be very busy today. Lizzie, love, go up with her and see that William behaves.' She turned back into the kitchen.

'What's Mama getting all excited about?' asked Mary Ann, pulling on her one stocking.

'I'm going to England,' said Henry bluntly.

'England?' Mary Ann's eyes glowed. 'I mean, I've know all year that you're going. But you are really truly going soon? This week?'

'In two days.'

'You boys have all the excitement,' said Mary Ann.

Elizabeth, meanwhile, had been watching her brother's face. 'You don't look very excited, Henry. Don't you want to go?'

Henry paused, rubbing his hand up and down the bannister rail. 'Well, we've always heard so much about England. About the towns and cities, the big churches … and all the people and carriages, and … and everything.'

'Well,' said Elizabeth, 'isn't that exciting?'

'But I've never been anywhere else; never even seen a carriage. The biggest building I've seen is the new stone store. I'll probably ask all the wrong questions and they'll think I'm stupid, and ... and I'll miss you all.' He kicked the bottom step.

'I think you're stupid, anyway,' flared Mary Ann. 'I'd give anything to go to England. Just think of seeing all those places, and buying clothes you could try on first.'

'You might even see snow,' said Elizabeth. 'Imagine a whole street of houses, big ones too. And remember the pictures of the cathedrals in Father's book: pillars so huge that people look like mice beside them.'

'And imagine roads that you can drive along without getting stuck in the mud!' said Mary Ann.

'Oh, you don't understand,' said Henry, pushing past Mary Ann, and going up the stairs. She stood and followed him into the boys' bedroom. Elizabeth followed more slowly. Richard was up and dressed. William was still in bed.

'Lizzie, Mama said you were to help me with William,' said Mary Ann.

'Only if he was difficult. But you're not difficult are you, William?'

Awed by this vote of confidence from his big sister, William just said, 'No,' and got out of bed.

Henry started taking his clothes out of the drawers and heaping them on his bed, but after a while he leaned on the window sill and gazed out over the inlet. Elizabeth joined him.

The mangroves on the other side of the inlet loomed grey-green through the lifting fog. Some Maoris were pushing a sleek, black canoe into the leaden water. Their muted voices carried across the river.

'They'll be going up the creek to inspect the eel traps. It's fun,' Henry said, 'but I may never go with them again.'

'They'll still be doing it when you return.'

'You might all be moved from here when I get back.'

'Papa says he's not going,' said Elizabeth.

'He says that, Lizzie, but he hasn't got much choice, has he? I think he is just trying to keep Mother's spirits up. She is terrified by the thought of moving. How could he make a living? If he wanted to stay here when they close it down, how could he pay rent? I doubt if he has much money saved, if any. *Te Karere* belongs to the mission; they'll send it down south and how would he get on without a boat?' He turned to look at Mary Ann and William, their five-year-old brother, who was standing quietly as she did up the buttons that attached his trousers to his jacket.

'William will be eight when I come back. Mary Ann will be twelve, same as you are now.'

'And Richard and William will probably have to go to England too, later on, if Father can afford it. So you'd better try not to sound afraid,' said Lizzie

Henry nodded and addressed his younger sister. 'You're probably right, Mary Ann, it will be exciting.'

'I know,' she snapped.

'What'll be exciting?' asked William.

'I've got to go to school — to England.'

'Oh, that place.' William dismissed it. ' But you haven't finished making our boat, Henry.'

'I'll ask James to finish it.'

Henry started folding up his clothes.

'There you are then,' said Mary Ann, patting William's chest. 'You go down with Henry and I'll dress Sarah.'

In the next room Sarah was already out of bed and washing her face and hands in the china bowl on the washstand.

Elizabeth sat on the edge of the bed and watched her sisters. Mary Ann gathered clothes for Sarah: a clean petticoat from the drawers and her dress from the chair where she had left it the night before.

'Found it!' she cried, waving her lost stocking. 'Sorry, Lizzie,' she had the grace to say. 'It was muddled with Sarah's things.'

'I'll dress Sarah if you like, while you tidy the beds,' Elizabeth offered.

'Sarah can almost dress herself now, can't you, love? You go to Lizzie and she'll help you. Dry your hands properly. And take your hairbrush and ribbon.'

Four-year-old Sarah had soon dressed herself with minimal help. She handed the hairbrush and ribbon to Elizabeth and turned her back. For such a small girl she had an abundance of hair and Elizabeth started to brush each long brown lock.

'Why does Henry have to go away?' asked Sarah. 'He goes to school here.'

'Because boys have all the luck; you'll soon learn that. We just sit at home and hem handkerchiefs,' said Mary Ann.

'I wish you wouldn't say things like that — not in front of Mama anyway.'

'Why ever not?'

'Because she has so much work to do: looking after us and organizing all the workers, teaching the school and seeing to the meals. Especially with Father away so often.'

Lizzie brushed Sarah's hair back from the temples and stroked it together into her hand. She put the brush down and picked up the ribbon.

'I don't see what that has to do with it. She doesn't complain.'

'No,' said Elizabeth quietly. 'So why do you?'

She wrapped the ribbon deftly around the lock of hair and tied the knot, then the bow.

'Oh, Lizzie, I can't be like you, so content. I want to get away and see new places and do exciting things.'

'I expect there are hundreds of girls in England saying exactly the same thing, and envying us. And probably hemming handkerchiefs too,' Elizabeth grinned. 'There, Sarah, off you go for your breakfast.'

She stood up and tucked her crutches under her arms. 'Right! To the handkerchiefs. Follow me!'

Mary Ann followed her, laughing.

CHAPTER 3

It was well past midday before *Te Karere* returned from *The Elizabeth* which was anchored in deeper water out in the Bay of Islands. A triangle of white sail hovered over the mangroves then the small cutter appeared round the bend of the inlet.

Elizabeth, Mary Ann and several of the Maori girls from the school, sat on the front lawn in the sunshine, hemming handkerchiefs. Mrs Kemp sat with them, trying to finish the shirts that she was making for Henry.

Mary Ann was the first to see the sail. 'Look, the boat!' she cried, jumping up. 'Hooray! The boxes! Mama, we can open them before tea, can't we, Mama?'

'For once I'll agree. I want to find the new clothes that should be coming for Henry. He'll need to pack them.'

Seeing the boat lower its sail and glide up to the jetty, Mr Nesbit, the carpenter employed on the building of the stone store, pushed his hammer into his belt and strolled down to the wharf. The two Maori men who worked for the mission, John Taua, Mere's husband, and Thomas Reo, came round from the gardens. They soon had the boat tied up and the cases unloaded.

All the children were excited. This only happened three or four times a year. It meant new clothes, letters, new school books, even presents if they had had a birthday since the last boat.

Mary Ann found it impossible to keep still and darted about, getting in everyone's way, until her father barked at her and sent her off to help with lunch for the men.

Elizabeth finished the handkerchief she was hemming and went into the kitchen. She could hear Mary Ann the minute she opened the door.

'Honestly, Mama, I don't know how you can wait to see what is in them.'

'I'll manage.'

'You did put *coloured* shoes, didn't you? In the order?'

'I did.'

'What colour do you think they'll be?'

'We'll just have to wait and see.'

'Wouldn't red be beautiful — or blue. What do you think, Elizabeth? I think blue; it would go with my blue sash.'

Elizabeth could see her mother was getting exasperated and put in a quick suggestion. 'Perhaps you could go and make a clear space for the boxes in the schoolroom. I can help Mama with the lunch.'

'See Papa eats his lunch quickly,' was Mary Ann's parting shot.

Her mother shook her head and took a deep breath. 'Thank you, Elizabeth, a very timely suggestion. Perhaps you could butter this.' She pushed a platter of sliced bread across the table to Elizabeth.

'She does go on a bit,' said Elizabeth, reaching for the plate of butter.

Within half an hour lunch was over and Mary Ann came to inform them that the boxes were waiting to be unpacked. She then dashed away to notify Mrs Shepherd and Mrs Edmonds, in their nearby houses.

By the time they had all gathered in the schoolroom Henry was busy levering the lid off the first case; it came apart with creaks as the nails bent. The moment had arrived. The women stood at hand to check their lists.

Mary Ann was allowed first pick. She took a large box from the first layer and opened it. The box contained a man's top hat. She lifted it out and stroked the furry surface.

'Ah! One man's black beaver hat,' said Mrs Kemp, ticking her list.

'Papa's new hat. Try it on, Papa,' squealed Sarah.

Mr Kemp placed it on his head with all solemnity.

'My turn next,' claimed William. He reached in with his eyes shut and pulled out a small box which he opened. 'Reels of sewing cotton,' he said in disgust.

'Yes, that's half for me and half for you,' said Mrs Shepherd marking her list.

And so they went on, crossing off each item as it appeared: socks; shoe ribbon; one dozen men's shirts, large size; fine calico; one dozen black silk men's handkerchiefs; bed ticking; six print dresses.

'For me, for me?' called Mary Ann.

'Two each, of course,' said her mother pulling one out of the bundle and giving it a shake. 'I hope they made them large enough. I asked that they be large, with plenty of tucks.'

'I wish you wouldn't, Mama,' Mary Ann complained. 'When they are new they look like a bunch of tucks and when they get to being the right size they're old and covered in stripes where the tucks have been let out. And look how old-fashioned they are. The latest thing is to have natural waists and full skirts — Mrs Busby told me — and she is the Governor's wife so she should know. It's quite out to have high-waisted dresses now. I expect they sent us old stock.'

'Well, I like them,' said Elizabeth, seeing how the complaints upset her mother.

'So do I,' Mrs Kemp agreed. 'High waists are a much daintier style for children.'

'Yes, but out of date,' muttered Mary Ann, under her breath.

Mrs Kemp ignored her and continued unpacking. 'Two pieces of brown holland.' She felt the material between her fingers, checking it for quality. 'Two dozen pairs of children's shoes, two to ten years.' The shoes kept on coming out and were handed to Richard who placed them against the wall, until they stood in a row right along the side of the room, all of black or brown. Mary Ann peered into the case but there were no more.

Henry levered the lid off a new case and it was William's turn again. He reached in and lifted out a cardboard box. He raised the lid and peeped in, then slammed it down quickly.

'Oh, come on, William,' said Richard, 'don't be childish.'

'I am a child so I'm allowed to be childish,' retorted William. He peeped under the lid again and giggled. 'You'll never guess in a million years.'

'William, hand it over,' ordered his mother, reaching for the box. She, too, lifted the lid but put it straight back down.

'How could they? It's really too bad of them.'

'What, Mama?' they chorused.

'It's only because we live so far away and can't send them back,' she complained to her husband.

'What, Mama?'

'Yes dear, what?' asked Mr Kemp, smiling.

Slowly, his wife lifted the lid and held out the box. It contained a pair of shoes. They were bright puce-pink, embellished with purple bows.

Mr Kemp's mouth lifted at the corners and Richard laughed outright. In a moment they had all joined in. All, that is, except Mary Ann and her mother who stood transfixed.

'You did ask me to put coloured in the order,' said Mrs Kemp. 'But I do think it is too bad of them.'

Mary Ann reached into the shoe box and picked one out. Elizabeth could see that she didn't know whether to laugh with the others or to cry.

'Perhaps,' said their mother faintly, 'we could remove the bows.'

'They probably made them for someone who changed their mind when they saw them,' said Elizabeth.

'And I don't blame them!' said young James, setting off fresh peals of laughter.

Mary Ann glared at them. 'Well, I think,' she said in a loud voice, using a phrase of Mrs Busby's, 'that they look vastly elegant!'

Elizabeth breathed a sigh of relief.

'How about the next box, Henry?' said Mr Kemp.

Soon all the cases had been opened and the contents sorted and checked. The last box was from the Church Missionary

Society, and contained the mail that had accumulated over several months at the society's office, awaiting shipment.

It was late afternoon before all the mail had been read, the new school stationery stacked on the shelves, and the new crockery taken into the kitchen to be washed and sorted.

'Father, can I come and help you with the boxes for the store now?' asked James.

'Can I come too?' pleaded Elizabeth. 'I can check the lists.'

'Right, James and Elizabeth can come with me; the rest of you can help here.'

Elizabeth picked up her crutches and followed. They went to the small shed that served as a store until the new one would be finished. Several unopened cases stood outside, containing the goods that were sent from the society as sale items. The men carried one inside and James levered off the top. Elizabeth was lifted onto the bench under the window, with the lists and a crayon for marking them off.

James handed out the first package, saying, 'One gross fish hooks, large.'

Elizabeth crossed it off the list as Mr Kemp tipped them into a box on the shelf marked FISH HOOKS LARGE, and reached for another package.

'Papa, now Henry's going, you won't have him to be your interpreter, will you?' said Elizabeth.

'No, I'll miss him. He's always had a better grasp of the language than I have. But then, I've improved a lot. James can come with me if I need him. He's eleven now.'

'A dozen pairs of scissors.' Before handing them on, James snipped at a piece of packing paper and seemed satisfied that they were sharp.

Elizabeth marked them off, repeating the statement.

'But Papa, I'm older than James and you've always said that I'm better at Maori than he is.'

'Not much,' growled James.

'Aye, and you're a lass,' replied her father bluntly.

'What difference does that make?'

'Well, it would not be seemly. We travel many miles and very rough ones at that. Even though he is younger, James is stronger than you.'

'Then it's because of my leg,' she snapped.

'No, love, don't always be ready to jump. It's as I have said. Even if you were fit and well, I would not take you.'

James gave his father a small bundle in a waterproof bag. 'Ten pounds saltpetre. What's that for?' he asked.

'For preserving meat.'

Elizabeth held the list up to the window. 'I can hardly see the words.'

'Yes, it's getting too dark. It's pointless going on now. Run up and get Thomas if you can find him, James. He can help me lift the other cases in overnight.'

James left on his errand and Elizabeth persisted with her father.

'Papa, my bad leg would not hinder you. I can go quite fast.'

Her father sighed. 'Lizzie, love, how can I make you understand? 'Tis not only your leg — though it would be a hindrance, and you've got to face up to that. No, the boys can help me and it's your job to help your mother.'

'But that's not …' she screwed her face into a frown.

'Not what?'

'Not God's work.'

'Well, I would say it was; but what are you trying to say?'

Elizabeth took a deep breath. 'Because if I were doing God's work he might make my leg better.'

Mr Kemp sighed. 'Oh, Lizzie, you can't barter with God.'

'Well, what can I do?' she asked desperately.

'Just go on praying, as we do.'

'But I do and nothing happens,' she protested.

'I'm sorry, Lizzie, but I haven't got an answer. Perhaps it's not what we want but what God wants that matters.' He lifted her down, then said urgently, 'But Lizzie, if my work is God's work, then your mother's is too. I could not do mine without her. When I return to a clean house and clothing and food and happy, well-instructed children, I thank God for her. And it is God's work for you to be her comfort, just as she is mine. Especially now when there will soon be another baby to care for. You can see that, can't you?'

'I suppose so,' she said. 'But, Papa, I do try.'

'I know you do, love.'

'It just seems so ordinary.'

'Most things are.'

Chapter 4

September, 1833

Dear Henry,

It is over a month now since you left. There is no boat here to send this letter on but I think it is as well to have it ready for when a boat comes, don't you? James asks me to say that he is sorry that he forgot to wave when the boat left; it was just that Oka came up to talk to them and when he turned back you had almost disappeared. He says that he did wave but you might not have seen him, or did you? I think it is a bit silly to ask you this because by the time the boat gets this letter to you in England it might be six months. And by the time you write back and get the letter on another boat it will be nearly a year before he gets an answer. But it seems to worry him so I have put it in. He's sorry anyway! I hope you had a good journey.

What is going on here? Much as usual, with Papa off on his tours, visiting the kainga up and down the coast. Sometimes he walks, sometimes he goes in Te Karere. I am sure he misses you but John Taua often goes with him now. Mere asked me to send you her love. I know that she means that very sincerely, Henry. She seems to think of you almost as her own son. In fact, she told me once that ever since she rescued you from drowning when you were a little boy, she thinks of you as partly hers.

Mama continues to worry about whether the committee is going to move us all. In fact she never stops worrying everyone: Papa, George Clarke, Mr Williams. They just have to make an appearance and she is asking them to write letters to the committee here, or to the Reverend Jowett in England at the C.M.S. office there. Poor Mama, I can understand it. Imagine trying to pack up and move with all us lot. Imagine having to leave this house. And having to live in tents and native huts until they get a new house built. And meeting new natives, all her old friends left behind. I don't think I would like it either.

James has got the idea into his head that he wants to be a farmer when he grows up. He is always talking about Mr Davis, over at Te Waimate, and the great job he is doing, breaking in new land for cultivation. I think Papa is very pleased that he is interested and is already talking about trying to purchase some land from one of the chiefs for any of you boys who want to be farmers. I can't see you wanting to do that though. Perhaps you'll be a teacher. What will any of us do? I hope you don't decide to stay in England. Please don't do that, Henry. I would miss you dreadfully.

1st December, 1833

At last a ship has come, The Elizabeth *again! My ship! She is leaving for Port Jackson tomorrow. I am finishing this letter in a rush, to tell you the great news. We have a new little brother who was born a month ago on the 26th of October. He is called Samuel Marsden Kemp, shortened to Sam of course. He is quite beautiful.*

Mama has not been too well since he was born, she looks very thin and tired and seems so sad, not at all as she usually is. Papa told me that she needs lots of rest and asked me to help look after Sam until she is better. That is no problem, in fact I love it. Every morning I bath him and change him into his day clothes. I wash his night clothes out by hand and hang them to dry before school starts. In the afternoon I amuse him and play with him. He has just started to smile a bit. I'm sure he knows me.

Mr Nesbit made him a wooden rattle. Sam tries to hold it but his fingers are too small, in fact his fingernails are hardly there. My main problem is that I cannot carry him about with my crutches. Mr Nesbit is very kind though, and if it is a fine day he comes and carries Sam, in his cradle, down by the river. Sometimes he takes him into the garden, or whenever he is working on the stone store, so that he gets some fresh air.

It is getting warmer now Christmas is only a few weeks away. I expect you are getting colder and colder. Mama keeps on worrying whether your clothes are warm enough.

Mere and Titohea Reo have been looking after the house and the native girls. James and Richard are both going over to school with Mr Brown at Paihia, as you used to, and coming home for weekends. Mary Ann sends her love and asks, 'What are clothes like in England now?' William is starting to write quite well. He wants to put a little on the end of this letter.

From your loving sister,
Elizabeth.

Dear Henry,

I hope you are well. I am well, so is the cat. James finished the boat, it sails well. I caught three fishes off the wharf on Tuesday.

Love from
William.

CHAPTER 5

A flight of wild ducks alighted on the surface of the river, skidding to a halt in a flurry of wings and water. Elizabeth dropped her sewing onto her lap and watched them. Richard Kemp and young Tamati Reo sat on the bank, their fishing lines drifting idly in the river. The ducks dipped and preened and flung up sparkling sprays of water.

'They're good to eat,' said Tamati, after watching them for a while.

'Mmm,' agreed Richard, 'but they're hard to catch. Except with a gun. How do Maori catch ducks?'

'I don't know.'

'Do they trap them or spear them like pigeons, or what?' persisted Richard.

'I don't know,' repeated Tamati. 'I've never seen them caught.'

'There must be a way.'

'I know how to catch weka,' Tamati volunteered.

'But they're not weka, are they? They're ducks.'

'There are weka over Rangitane,' said Tamati.

'But you know you're not allowed that far away,' Elizabeth cut in. ' Besides, it's Tareha's land.'

'I suppose so,' said Tamati. 'Pity, eh! Weka are easy to catch.'

The boys sat in silence for a while. Then Richard pulled up his line and examined the bait.

'They haven't even nibbled. There's nothing here,' he said, rolling up his line.

Tamati was lying back against a tree root looking up at the water-light dappling the branches.

'You ever seen Tareha?' Richard asked.

'No.'

'You seen him, Lizzie?' Tamati asked, turning his head.

'Not that I can remember.'

'Don't you think it's odd? We often hear about him but we've never seen him,' reflected Tamati. 'They say he's a giant.'

'Yes,' said Richard, 'Henry used to tell us terrible tales about him. I think he just made them up, like fairy stories.'

'My father did that too. He used to say, "Tareha will catch you with his great long arms and put you in a hangi and eat you!" Both the boys laughed.

Elizabeth looked doubtful. 'I don't know,' she said. 'Mama told me that Tareha was so big he couldn't get through the door of our house.'

'I've never seen anybody who couldn't get through a door, have you?' said Richard, scornfully.

'No. But Mama doesn't tell lies.'

'When we were little we believed them, but not now. I expect she was just telling a good story,' said Tamati.

'What if we did go over to Rangitane for weka? The river's the boundary to Tareha's land. We could stay on this side and

35

if we heard anybody come we could just run back quickly.'

'You aren't allowed,' said Elizabeth.

'No, I s'pose not,' said Richard. He turned his back on her and faced Tamati. 'Come on then, Tamati, we'll go up the river and see if they're biting up there.' They picked up their gear and walked down to the stepping stones that crossed the river.

'Now don't you go to Rangitane,' called Elizabeth. 'Papa will be furious if you do.'

'Who'd tell him?' taunted Richard.

'I would.'

'No, we're going up the river, aren't we, Tamati?'

Tamati nodded and grinned.

Elizabeth watched them gain the opposite bank and walk upstream to the bush. She did not quite trust them. But what could she do?

Elizabeth had a bad day. She had to unpick a length of sewing when she found that she had sewn it inside out. She dropped a cup and broke it. She cut her finger sharpening a quill pen and it bled on her new apron. Everything went wrong.

Later that afternoon as she was walking out to the cattle yard, to take a message to her father, she saw Richard and Tamati. They were with a group of Maori, coming down the far bank of the river. All the tensions of the day crystallized.

'I knew it,' she exploded. 'Those stupid boys.'

Hearing Elizabeth, her father looked up and followed her gaze.

'Tareha!' He dropped his tools and went to meet the party as they came over the stones.

Elizabeth gaped. Seeing the leader of the group standing beside her father, she knew that he must be at least seven feet tall, with a girth so enormous that she didn't even try to think what he must weigh.

Richard and Tamati had collapsed, panting, onto the grass. Mr Kemp looked at them dubiously, but addressed the chief. 'Welcome, Tareha. It is many years since you last visited us.'

'I do not like coming here,' he replied bluntly. 'The ghosts of the past rise before me. The mana of this river washed many war canoes when we went with Hongi, that great warrior. I still see them. If it were not for your son I would not be here.'

'Richard?'

'Aie, and this boy of Tamati Reo's. Have they not been taught that my land is my land? That my birds are my birds?'

'They have been taught.'

'Why is it then that they come onto my land and kill my birds?' He pointed to a man behind him who held up a bunch of dead weka.

Richard was still lying on the ground. He must have heard — as Elizabeth did — the sorrow in their father's voice.

'Is this correct, Richard?'

Richard mumbled into the grass.

'Stand up! You too, Tamati.'

They crept to their feet and stood with heads hung low.

'You both know your catechism. Tamati, what is the eighth commandment?'

'Thou shalt not steal.'

'Richard, the tenth?'

'Thou shalt not covet thy neighbour's house, nor his wife, nor his ox nor his ass…'

'Nor his birds. Say it!'

'Nor his birds,' they muttered in unison.

Mr Kemp turned to Elizabeth, 'Lizzie, go and fetch Thomas Reo. And bring my quince stick.' Then as an afterthought, 'No need to bother your mother.' He spoke again to the chief. ' I'm sorry this has happened, Tareha. They shall be beaten and shall also make retribution to you.'

'That is what you would do, wouldn't you? Beat little children, eh? No Maori would hit so small a thing!'

Elizabeth hobbled back to the house as quickly as she could while the men's voices continued in a rising tone of argument.

When she reached the front door her mother was already there. 'Lizzie,' she asked with agitation. 'Who is that talking with your father?'

'It's Tareha,' said Elizabeth.

'Oh, dear Lord, what does he want?'

'Richard has done something to annoy him, but don't worry. Papa said not to worry you with it; he can manage.'

'The silly boy.' She squeezed her apron between her hands.

'Tamati too,' said Elizabeth. 'Papa sent me to get Thomas.'

'He's in the kitchen.' Mrs Kemp turned back into the house. 'Thomas,' she called, toward the open door, 'come quickly. Those silly boys. It's Tareha!' She set off down the steps with Thomas following.

Elizabeth took up the long pliable quince stick that always stood, as a warning, in the corner by the door.

The heated voices of the two men could still be heard. The boys stood to one side as though forgotten. Tareha had turned his back on the group and was gazing down the inlet, his heavy voice speaking almost in lamentation.

'The only reason I leave you alone is because Hongi wished

it,' he was saying. 'What would he say now? Hongi, who lies unavenged because of you. He who righted every wrong with utu. It is you who have put such weakness into their knees and into their minds.' He gestured angrily towards the Maori pa which could be seen further down the inlet. 'You and your God. Aie, aie, aie,' he moaned. 'Why did he listen to you? Why?

'With him, life was worth something. So many battles. So much glory, aie, aie. Why did he protect you? You beaters of children, you bringers of disease, you destroyers of our ways.' He turned back to the group with such a bleak expression on his face that, for all the horror of his words, Elizabeth almost felt sorry for him — until he turned and saw Mrs Kemp, and his lips suddenly stretched wide in a mirthless smile.

'Ah, Mrs Kemp,' he said slowly. 'It is many years since we met. Perhaps you still live by our laws?'

With a sudden movement he grabbed Richard around the waist and swooped him up into the air, holding him horizontally above his head. It happened so quickly that everyone was bereft of speech.

'What I have I hold, Mrs Kemp. Isn't that the law you use?' he roared. 'I shall take him home and he shall work for me. Isn't that fair exchange, Mrs Kemp?'

Elizabeth stared up at Richard, terrified by his precarious position. His limbs swam through the air. She was astonished to see him smile and then shriek with laughter. Not just a timid giggle but a raucous screech that went on and on.

Tareha was as suprised as any one. He dropped his arms and held Richard level with his face. 'You are laughing?' he said in bewilderment.

Richard went on snuffling and wheezing.

Elizabeth knew what it felt like to get the giggles, however inappropriate. When the laughter kept on rising up to your head like bubbles that had to escape.

Tareha lowered Richard to the ground where he collapsed, snorting, into the grass. They all stood around, looking at him in amazement.

Mr Kemp was the first to find his voice. 'I shall bring him to your place to do some work in repayment,' he said.

Tareha looked puzzled. 'I do not want repayment,' he said. 'Beat your child if you wish.' He turned abruptly and strode toward the river crossing. 'Come!' he called to his followers.

The group from the mission stood and watched him go, not quite sure what had happened. They saw him pause on the opposite bank and look back. He gave orders to one of his men, who detached himself from the knot of people and came jumping back across the rocks, a flax kete in one hand. He came straight to Richard and thrust the kete into his hand. It was full of kumara.

'From Tareha, for the boy who laughed in the face of danger,' he said, then turned and leapt back across the river.

CHAPTER 6

They went back to the house. Richard and Tamati were taken to the schoolroom and the beatings duly administered. Mere led Mrs Kemp into the dining room and helped her onto one of the dining chairs. She rested one elbow on the table while her hand covered her eyes. She had gone an odd ashen colour and was shivering. Mere knelt beside her and rubbed her other hand, talking quietly. Elizabeth hovered near.

Finally Mrs Kemp spoke. 'Did you hear him, Mere? He said, "What I have I hold."'

'Yes, he couldn't mean it,' murmured Mere.

'Why did he say that? What was that about?' asked Elizabeth.

'It was about me,' said Mere unexpectedly. 'I was his slave once, captured in Hongi's war, many years ago. I ran away. I came to your mother and I asked her, if he came looking for me, to say, "What I have I hold". It is our rule. You see, if a runaway slave is found by anyone else, the slave is then that person's property. He was furious. He planned to take me as a slave wife as is sometimes done. The words were enough, but your father bought me as well. With a blanket, a shirt and an axe. That is what I am worth. Tareha took them. He was making the best of the situation, but his mana was damaged and he never forgot.'

'Could he have kept Richard like Mama kept you?'

'No, of course not. He wasn't a runaway slave.'

'He was a thief,' said Mrs Kemp.

'It still doesn't apply. Truly,' said Mere earnestly. 'Lizzie, see if Titohea is in the kitchen. She may have gone with Thomas and Tamati, but if she is there, ask her to make some more tea. Nobody drank the last pot.'

Elizabeth went through to the kitchen and found Titohea, Tamati's mother, obviously just as upset as Mrs Kemp, but taking it out on a large burnt pot which she was scouring with fierce strokes. Elizabeth delivered the message and returned to the front room. Her father was there with a firm hand on the shoulder of Richard, who sobbed as he apologized to his mother.

'Right! To your room now. Stay there and dwell on your foolishness until the morning.' Mr Kemp gave him a slight push towards the door.

Elizabeth listened to his slow feet ascending the stairs. What a fuss it had all caused. 'I should have stopped them this morning,' she muttered.

Her mother caught the words and turned on her abruptly. 'What do you mean, Lizzie? You knew they were going on this crazy expedition?'

'Well, not exactly.' Elizabeth faltered, surprised by the sudden fury in her mother's voice.

'Not exactly?' repeated her mother. 'Lizzie, if you had any idea of where they were going, you should have told us.'

'I didn't know, truly I didn't. They just hinted, and I couldn't have stopped them anyway.'

'Oh, you silly girl. Look at all the bother you have caused.'

'But, Mama …'

Her father intervened. 'Charlotte dear, it isn't Lizzie's fault. More likely mine.'

'Yours?'

'Yes, I've left Tareha alone all these years. Fear I suppose. But there should be no fear in the Lord's work. I shall go to him soon. I must try to understand him. He is obviously confused.'

Titohea came in with the tea and Elizabeth took the opportunity to escape out onto the verandah. Sarah was there, playing with her wooden doll, trying to tie a piece of rag around its head to resemble a bonnet. Elizabeth plonked herself down on the top step. She plucked a few heads from the lavender bush that grew by the step, crushed them in her hand, and threw them onto the path. Isaiah, the cat, sidled up and rubbed the top of his head against her hand. She lifted him onto her knee and buried her face in the warmth of his black fur. She felt furious and miserable at the same time. How could her mother accuse her when Richard had been the culprit? It was so unfair. Why had she to take responsibility for their behavior?

Footsteps came through the door behind her and she felt a small body sit down hard on the step beside her. It was William. 'Lizzie, will you hear my text? I've got to have it learnt for Sunday School tomorrow, but everybody's so disagreeable. Richard's shut himself in his room. Mama told me to go away for now and I can't find Mary Ann anywhere. Please?'

Elizabeth held out her hand for the scrap of paper, grateful to have something to occupy her mind. 'Alright, go ahead.'

William took a deep breath and stared straight ahead. 'God is love. And he who liveth in God … um … liveth in love …'

'Wrong way round,' said Elizabeth.

'Loveth in live?'

'Don't be silly. He who liveth in love, liveth in God.'

'And God in him,' concluded William triumphantly.

'Now, right through.'

'God is love, and he who liveth in love, liveth in God, and God in him.'

'Good, now once more.'

William repeated it.

Elizabeth returned the scrap of paper. 'You seem to know that.'

'But I don't know what it means.'

'It sounds like poetry. I like poetry,' said Sarah, as she wrapped her doll in a bit of old blanket and cradled it in the crook of her arm.

'Here, hand it back.' Elizabeth held out her hand. She read it twice. The words jigged before her eyes, making less and less sense the more she looked at them. How could God live in a person; he was much too big for that.

A thin wail came from the upstairs bedroom. It was Sam, and with a sense of relief, Elizabeth made his cry an excuse to go back inside.

As she hopped up the stairs, Mere came out of the dining room.

'You're going up to Sam?' she asked.

'Yes.'

'Good, I'll be up in a minute.'

Elizabeth found Sam disgruntled and just waking up. She

bent over the cradle and chatted to him to encourage a smile.

'There then, and did you have a lovely sleep? There's a nice smile.' It was aimless, loving prattle. 'Who's a lucky boy then? Up here all alone with no one to worry him then. Don't bother to grow up, Sammy, love. It's not worth it, not a bit. You just get into all the troubles in the world.'

She felt his damp napkins and started to undo the long cloth tapes that held them in place.

'If your only worry is wet pants, it's not too bad, eh? You don't get blamed for things other people do, do you, poppet? That's right then, there's a lovely smile. Blow these tapes.' She picked at the tight, damp knot. 'And it's not fair, is it, love? Not fair at all, saying it was my fault.' She kept up an even murmur but a hint of bitterness crept into her voice. 'I do try, Sammy, honest I do, and now I get blamed for something I didn't even do.' Sam's face fell as he caught the distress in her voice. 'But Sam's alright. Mama loves Sam. Lizzie loves Sam. Everyone loves Sam. And poor old Lizzie will have to look after herself, won't she? But I think Sam loves Lizzie, doesn't he? After all, she looks after him, doesn't she? Yes, I'm sure Sam loves Lizzie, even if Mama doesn't.'

A faint sound caused her to look up. Mere was standing on the other side of the cradle.

'Oh Lizzie,' she said, 'don't feel like that. It wasn't your mother talking just now, it was her worry.'

'Perhaps,' said Elizabeth, her face still and distant.

'Of course it was,' said Mere. 'No one blames you. Not even your mother really. Everything seems to upset her these days. I'm sure she'll get over it. When all her worries are over. Be patient, Lizzie, just be patient.'

CHAPTER 7

March 1834

Dear Family,

I write to you all together because I can think of you standing around the box when it is unpacked, reading my letter aloud. How I miss you all and my friends too. Send my regards to John and Mere and to Thomas and Titohea and their families.

I have been working hard at school and Reverend Tacy who, as you know, I was named after, takes a proprietary interest in me and has been pleased with my marks. He is a very nice man which, you will realize, goes with the name. I am not top of the class but I am not bottom either.

Mr Esmond, the geography teacher, got me and two of the other boys to address the class on countries we had visited. Doncaster talked about India and Mason about Africa. I showed them the weaving and the bone tiki that Mere and John gave me, and sang some chants. I think they were quite impressed that I could speak the language. Regarding which, the Reverend Tacy had to go to Cambridge recently, to a gathering of clergymen. He took me with him to see Professor Lee who is a professor of languages. Apparently he has done much work on studying the Maori tongue. He told me that I am a unique person, because I am the first person he has met who can speak both English and Maori fluently. Hongi and Waikato, the Maoris he had met when they visited England, had both learnt some English. And the missionaries have learnt some Maori. But I was the only one who knew both. So, dear brothers and sisters, we are unique in this world. I spent the whole afternoon with him while Reverend Tacy attended his meeting; we had tea and muffins by the fire in his room, and chatted. He was much interested in all I had to tell him.

Mary Ann, you do ask me impossible questions but all I can tell you is that high waists are hardly seen any more, except on some old ladies. Skirts are very full and gathered and sleeves are big and puffed out on people who are trying to be fashionable. Is that enough?

Aunt Ann is a peach. Whenever she comes to Norfolk she brings me a great basket of fruit and baking and some extra good toffee she makes. Which all goes to cheer up the school food which is not very interesting but which could be called solid, I suppose.

It continues to be very cold. Several times we have had snow but it does not stay long. One week it was exceedingly cold and the river froze! You cannot conceive what it was like. Imagine the river at home suddenly going hard and smooth and us being able to walk on it. I tried to slide around but spent more time on my backside than on my feet, I am sad to report. Though there are signs that spring is on its way.

My cough is a bit better, you will be glad to hear, Mama. The matron of the school is very kind and when we are not well she gets a brick heated in the oven and wraps it in a cloth and puts it in our bed. It is very cosy on these cold nights.

I must finish this letter now as it is bedtime and I must send it away tomorrow. I think of you all often and, God willing, I will come back to you as soon as I possibly can.

Much love from Henry.

July 1834

Dear Henry,

It was lovely to get your letter and to hear all your news. What can I tell you that has happened here? There has been a bad outbreak of whooping cough. Quite where it came from, nobody knows. The natives have had it badly and several died. We have all had it too. Richard probably had it the worst but, though he still coughs at night, he is getting better slowly. Luckily, baby Sam only had a mild bout. Though it seems to be hanging on for a long time.

Mere, by the way, has taken over the complete running of the infant school. That has removed that burden from our mother, and she is now able to concentrate on the older girls.

Father has succeeded in buying some land. The Missionary Society has helped. They realize that it is incumbent on them to provide some future work for all of us, the children of the missionaries, as, when we come to the age of sixteen, they are *no longer responsible for giving our parents an allowance for us. James is so excited, he talks of nothing else.*

Father has another project also. He is planting an orchard, where the old cattle yards used to be. He has fenced it and dug it all over. The soil looks very rich, probably from the years of cattle droppings. Trees have been sent over from Australia, and we now have pears and apples, peaches and plums, lemons and oranges, all planted. We are hoping for a few fruit next year and lots more in the following years.

Mama, I'm afraid, does not take much interest. She is still deeply worried about the prospect of moving, and probably thinks that we will not be here to eat the fruit. Perhaps she is right to worry; the local committee is still pursuing the idea — though several people have written to them on our behalf. Even the old chief Tupe at Matangirau. He wrote a lovely letter asking for Papa to be left here. Papa is, however, always an optimist. He tells Mother that he will resign and just refuse to go, and that if they wish to close the station he will apply to rent the house, and will farm the 'children's land' as he calls it.

The others all send their love. Mary Ann thanks you for your fashion notes, and still envies you. James and Richard, as usual, go over to Paihia each week. William goes to Mere's school, and Sarah starts there next year. I help Mama, and look after Sam. Titohea does most of the cooking. So we carry on, much as usual.

Look after yourself, and come back to us safely.

From your loving sister,

Elizabeth.

CHAPTER 8

Elizabeth was not fond of Saturdays. She was a creature of habit with an orderly mind, and liked everything to take place in its due order. Weekdays had their routine, woven around necessity and schoolwork. Likewise Sunday, with time regulated by church services and Sunday School. Anything might happen on Saturdays, but they were odd and often boring.

On just such a boring Saturday Sarah grabbed Elizabeth's hand and said, 'Hana is going home to her kainga, down the river. Mama says I can go too, if you will come along to look after me. You will come, won't you? Please, Lizzie.'

Elizabeth considered briefly. It was something to do. 'Alright, if Mama doesn't want me to look after Sam.'

Mrs Kemp gave the girls permission to go. Hana was one of the teenaged girls who had finished her schooling and was now learning to do housework with Mrs Kemp.

'But be quick,' said their mother. 'Hana's brother is already here. Take a kete of corn for her mother as a gift. There is a boxful in the kitchen. Quick!'

Sarah filled the kete and they hurried through the gate. Sarah waved to Hana and her brother, Piripi, down on the foreshore, waiting by a small canoe. 'We can come,' she shouted.

The voyage down the inlet was fast and exhilarating. The canoe leapt upon the chop of the receding tide as it was guided skilfully to avoid the shallows and logs. Terns swooped and dived about them and several women picking cockles on a sandbank straightened their backs and waved to them.

It was not far to the kainga where Hana's family lived. The canoe ran up onto a small beach where several children played with a dog and some chickens.

A group of young women were sitting on the sandhills. They crowded around Hana, admiring the new dress she had made and feeling the material, talking and pressing noses.

Elizabeth followed as they walked to the nearby whares.

Sarah tugged at her hand. 'Can't I stay here and play?' she begged.

'Perhaps you'd better not.'

But Hana had heard, and turned back. 'Of course she can play,' she said imperiously. She was now on her own territory. 'Run and play, Sarah. Tui, keep an eye on her,' she called to the oldest girl on the beach. 'Come on, Lizzie, I want to show you something. Sarah will be alright.'

Elizabeth hesitated. Mama had sent her to look after Sarah. But Tui was there. And she knew it was polite to go and greet Hana's mother first. She followed the others to the village. After giving the corn and receiving thanks she was offered a large bundle of cut flax to sit on. From there she watched Hana's grandmother scraping and rolling the finest of flax fibres, all the while explaining to Elizabeth how they prepared it for the weaving of a fine cloak. Normally Elizabeth would have been fascinated, but when an hour had passed since she left Sarah on the beach, she felt on edge. Her mother's instructions, to care for Sarah, kept repeating in her mind.

The old kuia had finished explaining and was now grumbling, 'These young things, they don't want to learn now,' she said. 'They tell me, "We can get blankets from the Pakehas now and they are warmer." Blankets, huh! Whoever saw a blanket as good as a good flax cloak? Some day, when they can't get blankets, then they will know.'

Elizabeth was hesitant to interrupt and appear rude, but eventually her anxiety was too much. She reached for her crutch and tried to get up. 'Excuse me, but I think I had better see if Sarah is alright.'

'Hana will go and see, won't you, Hana?' said her mother, putting a detaining hand on Elizabeth's shoulder. Hana ran off towards the beach. Elizabeth watched her go with mixed feelings. Even the relief of knowing Sarah was safe wouldn't banish the nagging guilt, or the annoyance that she hadn't been able to choose for herself.

In a few moments Hana reappeared. 'They're fine,' she said.

But Elizabeth was glad when a short time later Piripi appeared.

'The tide's turning,' he announced. 'We'd better go soon if I am to get you home in time.'

Elizabeth got up with alacrity and thanked the old lady for letting her watch. It didn't take them long to get back to the beach. Elizabeth looked about, but there was no sign of Sarah.

Hana called out, 'Sarah! Sarah, time to go home!'

A small naked girl picked herself up from the beach and ran towards them. She was covered with a fine coating of sand, like all the other children. Elizabeth realized, with a shock, that it was Sarah.

'Where are your clothes?' asked Hana. 'We're in a hurry. We're late.'

Sarah pointed to a tree. Hana ran and pulled Sarah's clothes off the branch where they had been hung out to dry.

Piripi dragged the canoe to the water's edge.

'Sarah,' growled Elizabeth, in a low voice. 'What are you doing like that?'

'Like what?' asked Sarah, looking down at herself.

'Taking your clothes off. Covered in sand. What on earth will Mama say?'

Elizabeth started brushing it off with swift, hard strokes. Hana came back with the clothes and Elizabeth helped her dress with speed. Hana found her shoes and socks and pushed them into Sarah's hands.

'You can put those on in the canoe,' she ordered.

Piripi held the canoe steady. The girls stepped in and settled themselves. Piripi pushed the canoe well out before leaping in himself.

It took Sarah most of the way home to sort out her shoes and socks and get them onto the right feet. She had just completed her task when they rounded the last bend and came in sight of the settlement.

Elizabeth sat quietly throughout the voyage, taut with anxiety, her mind in a turmoil. Mama was going to blame her if she found out that Sarah had been playing naked. Should she ask the others not to mention it? Surely they wouldn't, anyway. Perhaps it was better not to say anything and hope that nothing would be said.

When they reached the house, everyone was gathered in the dining room for supper. They slipped into their seats as Hana apologized.

'I'm sorry, Mrs Kemp, I talked too much and didn't notice the sun sinking so low.'

Mrs Kemp nodded and lowered her head as Mr Kemp said grace. She took the lid off a big tureen and ladled the soup into dishes which were passed up the table. She put the lid on again.

'Well, Sarah, did you have a good afternoon?'

'Lovely,' said Sarah. 'I swam and swam.'

Elizabeth groaned inwardly.

Her mother looked suprised. 'Swam?' She looked at Hana and Elizabeth in turn. 'I thought she was going to the village with you.'

'She played on the beach with the other children.' Hana explained, reaching for a piece of bread. 'I got a big girl to watch her.'

'But swimming. How did you get your clothes dry?' Mrs Kemp asked Sarah. 'I hope you're not sitting in damp clothes.'

'Oh, no,' said Sarah blithely. 'I didn't get them wet. Well, not much. I took them all off.'

There was a moment's stunned silence. Mary Ann giggled.

'Took them off?' repeated Mrs Kemp, slowly. 'Oh, Sarah.'

'I wasn't there,' said Elizabeth, without thinking.

'Obviously,' snapped her mother. 'And you should have been, shouldn't you? You were sent to look after her but you just went and left her alone.'

'She wasn't alone,' Elizabeth lamented.

Hana looked on in bewilderment. 'The other children had no clothes.' She faltered. 'How could you swim with clothes?'

Mr Kemp stepped in quickly. 'Well, I don't see that any harm's done, love. It does seem the most sensible way to swim, and Sarah's only four.'

'Five,' his wife corrected him. 'No harm perhaps, as you say. But how can I teach them? How can they be ladylike? And if we go to Tauranga it will be worse. They will run wild like little savages.'

'Charlotte, dear,' said Mr Kemp. 'Sarah is not a little savage. Neither are Hana's people. It was the best way.'

Mrs Kemp stood up, tears starting in her eyes. 'You don't understand. Oh, how can I?' She pulled out her handkerchief and dabbed her eyes. The children watched, silent. They had never before seen their mother so upset. Suddenly she said, 'Excuse me,' and left the room.

Everyone sat in silent embarrassment. Richard dropped his spoon and it clattered against the dish.

'You must excuse your mother,' said Mr Kemp. 'She is overwrought and worried that we may have to move. I'm sorry, Hana, it's not your fault. Come on, children, eat your soup.'

The others started but Hana sat looking at her plate.

Elizabeth noted that she had not been included in her father's apology. Perhaps he also considered her at fault.

'Mr Kemp,' said Hana finally, 'Mrs Kemp taught me from the Bible about Adam and Eve. It was only when the devil talked to them that they were ashamed of being naked and hid from God.'

Mr Kemp looked at his soup. 'Yes, Hana, you are right,' he said slowly. 'I am sure when Mrs Kemp stops to think she will see that you are right. We are all brought up with odd ideas. Your people have them, and we have them too.'

As soon as she could, Elizabeth went to bed and cried bitter tears into her pillow. Everything was so unjust. However much she tried to help, the whims of other people thwarted her intent and she received the blame.

Perhaps tomorrow all would be forgotten and she could start again.

Chapter 9

The next day, Sunday, followed its comforting pattern of worship, meals, Sunday School, letter-writing and, for Elizabeth, helping with Sam. Although nothing more was said about the previous day, there was a tension that could not be fixed. Everything that Mrs Kemp said was relevant to the occasion but with no associated chat, which gave the impression that she had withdrawn from them.

Shortly before the morning service was due to start, James and Elizabeth went up to the church, a small, white plastered building on the hill overlooking the settlement. The windows and doors were painted green, the roof shingled. A clock was set in the gable end and told the time to any in the valley who cared to glance that way. A flagpole, flying the Union Jack, stood beside the building. Barren, bracken-covered hills rose behind.

James's task was to ring the handbell. The sound shattered the peace and sent a crowd of seagulls up in a squawking mass. They wheeled around the calm waters of the basin, uttering plaintive cries.

Elizabeth sat on a small bench by the door, ready to hand out the service and hymn books, recently printed in Maori, to those who required them.

Several groups of people started to wend their way toward the church. They came from the two pas, one on each side of the inlet, and from the cluster of houses that formed the mission. They were a motley collection. The missionary families were a monochrome of black, grey and white, except for the odd flash of colour in the sashes and bonnet ribbons of the little girls.

The Maori, however, supplied much greater variety. Many stayed with their native costume and came in feathered and patterned cloaks. Others had taken to European dress in its more colourful aspects. Red baize shirts and striped cotton trousers, bought from the store, were in favour. The headwear was equally varied, from straw bonnets and beaver hats to feathered topknots. Sailors' caps and bright tartan Scotch caps, bought from the store, completed the mix.

Mr Kemp arrived first, hurrying. He had several books and papers under his arm and glanced at the clock as he passed. 'My goodness, is that the time? I should have been here ten minutes since.'

'I put out the benches and lit the candles, Father,' said James.

'Good lad, good lad,' muttered his father, hastening inside.

The rest of the Kemp household soon followed, Mary Ann first, with her pink and purple shoes peeping, like a pair of exotic birds, from beneath her dress. She tugged a reluctant William by the hand.

Inside, the church was pleasant and light, the walls plastered and painted white, the ten small window surrounds in green.

Several well-made wooden pews, recently finished by Mr Nisbet, stood at the front. Behind were rows of plain wooden benches.

From the doorway, Elizabeth was able to see that William had escaped from Mary Ann and made for his favourite seat on the first row of benches, just behind the pews. She knew from experience that he liked to sit there right beside a window where he could look down on the buildings and the inlet below, and see the boats and the birds. She could see no harm indulging him in this; it kept him from wriggling. Once she had finished her job, Elizabeth eased along the bench beside him. She sat down and handed him her crutches. 'Here, prop them in the corner,' she commanded, 'and open the window; it's hot.'

He grinned and obeyed her.

The church soon filled with people and their father began the service in a loud, strong voice, reading from the Book of Common Prayer, first in English, then in Maori. '"If we say we have no sin, we deceive ourselves and the truth is not in us. But if we confess our sins, he is faithful and just to forgive us our sins and to cleanse us from all unrighteousness.

'"*Ki te mea tetahi kua matau a hau ki a ia a, kahou e pupuri i ana ture he tangata teka ia, Ka hore hoki te pouo i roto i a ia. Ko te tangata a pupuri ana i tana kupu kua tino rite pu I a ia te aroha o te atua ma konei tatou ka matau ai kei roto ta tou I a ia.*"'

There was a general murmur of assent. Thomas Reo stood up and sang the first line of a hymn. Once they recognized the hymn, the congregation took up the second line with a great roar of sound that lasted to the end. There was no such thing as *pp* — it was all *fortissimo,* each trying to outdo the other.

Mr Kemp stepped forward again. '"Dearly beloved brethren, the scripture moveth us in sundry places to acknowledge and confess our manifold sins and wickedness.'"

Elizabeth sighed. She had not meant to commit any wicked-nesses this week but they seemed to have descended upon her. She hadn't meant that the boys should be captured by Tareha. But how could she have stopped them? She had meant to look after Sarah. But hadn't wanted to appear impolite.

The congregation shuffled to its knees.

"'Almighty and most merciful Father we have erred and strayed from thy ways like lost sheep…'"

Elizabeth glanced sideways at William. He was licking patterns on the back of the pew in front. They showed up clearly on the new wood. Elizabeth frowned and shook her head. She was rewarded with a big grin. She shook her head again but couldn't help smiling back. William seemed to take this as approval and turned back to his licking. If she reproved him he might create a scene. He wasn't really doing any harm to anybody. Best to just leave him. She watched him work his way along the woodwork towards the window. When William reached the end he looked back along his artwork and she saw, to her horror, that his head was going to touch the crutches. Then, as if in slow motion, one of them began to slide.

"'Forty years long was I grieved with this generation and said …'"

William tried to right himself but only succeeded in toppling over and landing, with a crash and a yelp, under the bench. The crutch continued on its downward path, banging the window sill, the bench, then the floor.

Their father's voice faltered for a second then continued strongly. "'It is a people that do err in their hearts, for they have not known my ways.'"

William looked as though he was down in a pit. Heads all around peered down at him.

Mrs Kemp turned from the pew in front. 'Keep him in order!' she hissed at Elizabeth, shaking her head. 'You're right beside him.'

William struggled to his feet and sat on the bench again. He bent to retrieve the crutches.

'Leave them,' whispered Elizabeth. 'And sit still.'

William sighed and turned to the window.

CHAPTER 10

It was a fresh, clear morning. Rain in the night had washed the air and the plants, dampening the ground and leaving clumps of grass heavy with raindrops. Elizabeth picked her way across, trying to avoid the larger tufts which could leave the hem of her dress damp for the rest of the day. She had a small flax basket containing Sam's washed clothes which she wanted to hang out before school started.

She was worried about Sam. Probably without reason, Elizabeth told herself. He was over his mild dose of whooping cough. But he was not happy. She could see that. She asked her mother to have a look at him, but she had not appeared unduly concerned and the instructions were to wrap him warmly and keep him in the house. Though Elizabeth had followed these directions she still felt uneasy. Why was he so pink? Why so lethargic? He barely lifted an arm or turned his head. Had her mother not noticed?

When Elizabeth reached the schoolroom behind the house, the other pupils had all gathered: a mixture of children belonging to missionaries, workers and Maori from the nearby pa. She undertook her usual task helping Mere with the primary pupils: to write the copy for the day onto the blackboard.

'*F* today. Does that suit you all?' she asked. There was a general mumble of agreement. She picked up the chalk and carefully, in her best writing, copied from the book:

'*F f* Fair words are often used to hide bad deeds.

Few do good with what they have gotten ill.'

As she wrote the down strokes of ill, she suddenly thought of Sam. Perhaps he was really ill and nobody was with him. Though Titohea was there, in the kitchen. Surely she would go to him if he cried. She pulled herself together and started on the next row of copy.

'*G g* Great minds and small means ruin many men:'

Forgetting to write the second line of copy, Elizabeth sat down at her desk and took out her arithmetic book, but she looked blankly at the page. Suppose he was lying up there coughing or sneezing. She tried to concentrate on the problem in her book: 'In four hundred and sixty-five hundredweights and twenty-nine pounds of copper, how many pounds? And what would it cost at 21 pence per pound?'

Elizabeth looked out of the window. It was a beautiful day. The bees flew around the last of the Michaelmas daisies. She glanced across at her mother. For the first time Elizabeth noticed how tired she looked. How she stopped to straighten her back before moving onto the next child. Elizabeth's page was still empty when she reached her side.

'But you haven't done anything.'

'I can't, Mama. I'm too worried about Sam. Can I go and see him?'

Her mother sighed. 'Well, I can see I'm not going to get any work out of you until you do.'

Elizabeth jumped up gratefully and left the room. Mrs Reo was in the kitchen preparing vegetables.

'Mama says I may go and see if Sam's alright,' Elizabeth explained.

'Don't wake him. He was crying but he seems to have gone to sleep now.'

Elizabeth limped up the stairs, hanging onto the bannister rail for support. She opened the door and went in. The cradle stood beside the bed.

Sam was lying on his back, eyes wide open. When she bent over him he did not move his head. But his eyes turned beseechingly towards her. A small frown wrinkled his brow. Sweat dotted his face, and around his mouth the skin was pale, almost blue. Elizabeth could see that each inward breath was an effort.

She had never seen him like that before. So still and yet with such a wild look in his eyes, as though completely puzzled by what was happening to him. 'Sam, dear, what's the matter?' she whispered in alarm.

His eyes rolled towards her, pleading! He uttered small panting, grunts.

She hesitated, wondering whether to pick him up. No, she needed help. Hopping to the top of the stairs, she shouted, 'Mrs Reo! Mrs Reo, please come quick.'

Mrs Reo's head appeared through the door below the stairs. 'What's the matter?'

'It's Sam. There's something wrong with him.'

Mrs Reo ran up the stairs and knelt beside the cradle. She picked Sam up abruptly. He drew in a large gulping breath and his head waved in the air as though his neck could not support it.

'It's his chest, his breathing. Sit down,' she ordered.

Elizabeth perched anxiously on the edge of the bed as Mrs Reo placed the baby against her chest. 'Hold him upright like that. Let his head rest on your shoulder. I'll go and get your mother.'

Elizabeth sat still, the small damp bundle that was Sam held against her chest, his soft fuzzy hair tickling under her chin. A heart was thumping between them. She didn't know whether it was Sam's or her own. She could feel every tight breath and wheeze and the moist warmth of him soon seeped through her clothing. It seemed as though ages passed before she heard the murmur of voices ascending the stairs.

Her mother came in and knelt beside her, placing an ear against Sam's chest. She looked up at Elizabeth's anxious face.

'It's a touch of bronchitis or asthma. Don't worry, love, he'll come right.' She stood up and took the baby from Elizabeth. 'We'll take him down by the stove. Then we can get some steam around him. That's the best thing for tight chests.

'Titohea, you bring the cradle. Lizzie, get him a change of clothes. He's damp through.'

Elizabeth felt reassured. Her mother always knew what to do. She would soon have him better. Quickly, she gathered the clean clothes and followed her mother and Mrs Reo down to the kitchen.

The cradle was by the fire. Sam was propped up against a large cushion. Mrs Reo was tipping water into the pot that hung on a hook over the flames. Elizabeth placed the clothes on the table.

'Thank you, dear. Now get me a cold damp cloth to wipe his face. It is a good thing you went up to look at him. I didn't think that he looked so sick earlier.'

'He'll be alright though, won't he?' asked Elizabeth, wringing out the cloth and handing it to her mother.

'Of course, but he's very little.' She took the damp cloth and wiped the beads of sweat from his brow. 'Titohea, I'll get you some of those eucalyptus leaves to put in the pot. Miss Marsden sent them from Port Jackson. She said they were good for chests. Lizzie, you'd better go back to the classroom.'

'But, Mama …'

'Mere has all the children on her own. That's the best help you can be at the moment. When they have finished their writing you can read to them from the encyclopedia. We finished conchology yesterday. I think it's Cortez next.'

'Can't I stay?'

'Now go along, please, dear. Send two girls in for the lunch. I don't want them all in here. Tell them they can go home after lunch.'

'Can I come and see him?'

'Yes, but only you. Oh, I wish your father was here.'

At lunchtime there didn't appear to be any improvement. Sam didn't cry; he just looked about with imploring eyes. Sometimes he dozed, but soon awoke with a short dry cough that seemed to cause him pain. Tears welled up and ran down his cheeks. Elizabeth sat beside him, his tiny hand clutched around her finger like a bird's claw.

'Mama, there must be something else we can do.'

'We can pray,' said her mother.

Elizabeth shut her eyes. 'Please, God,' she prayed silently.

'You've got to make Sam better. He's only little. He can't help himself. Don't worry about me any more. I can get along. Help Sam, please. He can't understand. Don't you see that?'

She opened her eyes. Nothing had changed. The fire crackled in the grate. Steam rose from the pot and Sam still looked at her through half-closed eyes.

The afternoon dragged on. Elizabeth could not stay in the kitchen all the time. The dampness and heat and smell of eucalyptus were suffocating. She went out to sit on the verandah and to gaze blankly at the grey sky and water. The day, which had begun so well, had become still and ominous. The boys were playing with a ball, leaping and calling in the flat air.

After the evening meal Elizabeth took Sarah up to her bedroom and saw to her preparations for bed.

'Why aren't I allowed in the kitchen?' asked Sarah.

'Because Sam's ill. He's got a cough.'

'I wasn't kept in the kitchen when I had a cough. Why doesn't he go to bed?'

'He's in the cradle down there. It's warmer.'

'I liked people coming to see me when I was in bed with a cough.'

'Oh, stop chattering Sarah. Just remember to ask God to help Sam, in your prayers.'

'Did you pray for me when I had a cough?'

'No, you weren't very bad. Now say your prayers and get into bed.'

'Is Sam very bad? Is he going to die?' asked Sarah.

'Of course not. God wouldn't let him, would he?'

'He lets other people die.'

'Oh, be quiet,' said Elizabeth roughly, surprised by a tremor in her lip. She bundled Sarah into bed and blew out the candle, then turned and limped to the top of the stairs.

William was playing with his Noah's ark in the hall below, by the light of the guide lamp which always stood at the window. Elizabeth sat on the top step, her head in her hands, almost afraid to go back to the kitchen. William was muttering to himself as he gathered his animals from various parts of the room.

'Then the horses came, gallopy, gallopy, gallopy, berum, berum, berum …'

He bounced them across the room to the safety of the ark. 'Then the sheep came, baa, baa, baa …' He trotted them from under the table. 'Then the goats came down from the mountain.' He clambered up the stairs below her and she saw that he had placed several animals on the landing. Seeing her feet, he looked up, 'Oh! you're there. You can be God sitting in heaven, watching.'

Was God watching? Were people just toys to him? Lizzie wondered.

'I'm not playing,' she told William.

'Alright,' he said cheerfully. 'Then the goats came down, jumpity, jumpity, jumpity …' He thumped a goat from step to step. 'Bother!' He held the animal up. 'His leg's broken. He couldn't have been very strong. Can you mend him?'

'Not at the moment.'

'But he won't stand up,' William complained, coming up the steps and handing her the pieces.

'I'll get a pin and stick it in for now. Go into the dining room.' Elizabeth followed him to the sewing table in the corner and found a pin. Mary Ann was sitting there reading in the circle of yellow light under the lamp.

'How's Sam?' she asked.

'I don't know. I've been putting Sarah to bed. I'll go and see in a minute.'

Elizabeth pushed the pin into the goat and stood him on the table. He leant to one side but stayed erect. 'There, that'll do for now, but treat him carefully or he'll not last long.'

The words echoed in Elizabeth's head: *he'll not last long, he'll not last long.*

She glanced across at the kitchen door, afraid, but she knew she had to go in.

Her mother was standing by the cradle, head down, with her hands over her face. The cushion had been pulled out and thrown to the floor. Sam was lying flat. At the sound of the door, Mrs Kemp lifted a pale, stricken face. 'Sam's dead,' she said.

They stood, just looking at each other until the silence became oppressive.

'It's your fault,' Elizabeth said finally.

Her mother looked at her in astonishment.

But all the pent-up resentment and anger, at the times she had been blamed for the other children's bad behavior, erupted, and she lashed out. 'If only you'd looked at him this morning when I told you. And I told you yesterday that he had a cold, but you didn't take any notice. Don't you care?'

'Of … of course,' stuttered her mother. 'But we have to accept the will of God,' she added.

Elizabeth could feel the anger welling up inside, the heat rising to her face. 'What a stupid God!' she said bitterly. 'And what a stupid will.'

She couldn't bear the look of horror on her mother's face.

She had to get away. She opened the back door then slammed it shut as she swung out into the night. Limping blindly along the path towards the river she stopped abruptly beside the henhouse. *Where am I going?* She could hear the sounds of the hens fluffing their feathers and crooning as they settled for the night. The only other sound was the river slipping by with a soft sibilant whisper. The stars blazed fiercely in the still, night sky. Elizabeth looked up angrily.

'Why didn't you save him?' she said quietly, 'It wouldn't have made any difference to you.'

The stars still winked, the river rippled and the hens clucked gently to themselves.

'I don't even think you're there,' she shouted defiantly into the sky.

But no denial came.

'There's nothing, nothing ...' The words dissolved into the night. 'And Sam won't ever come back.'

Elizabeth felt the dark absence of hope. Her anger turned to misery and, dropping down into the long, dew-wet grass, she leant against the henhouse wall and wept.

CHAPTER 11

The wind blew across the churchyard in sharp gusts. The ladies clutched their shawls against their arms and prayed that their bonnets would stay in place. Each squall brought a sharp patter of raindrops or a few dried leaves spinning off the trees. The group stood around the hole, the heap of earth, and the small box that was Sam.

The Reverend Williams stood at the head of the grave, his surplice whipping in the wind. He held the pages of his book with both hands to stop them flapping, but the corners still fluttered with each gust.

"'Man that is born of woman hath but a short time to live. He cometh up and is cut down like a flower. He fleeth as it were a shadow and never continueth in one stay.'"

The men lowered the box into the earth and Mr Williams bent to gather a handful of crumbled clay. Elizabeth turned away and looked down at the house and at the cattle eating the yellow stubble where the oats had been cut. The smoke from the chimney blew wildly about the house and garden.

It will be warmer by the fire for my cold feet, she thought.

She glanced back at Mr Williams as he started to speak again.

'"… and shall lead them unto living fountains of water, and God shall wipe away all tears from their eyes."'

Elizabeth had a momentary vision of Sam's face and the tears welling up in his eyes as he coughed. Her lips tightened and she saw her mother looking at her. She pretended not to see, and looked down at the grave. Her anger of the night had dissipated, but a cold regret had taken its place. Words, once spoken, were said forever and she did not know how to take hers back.

In a few minutes it was all over. Their friends and neighbours, who had gathered to give them support, passed Mr and Mrs Kemp one by one. They offered condolences before walking down the path to the house. Elizabeth was the last to leave. She glanced back. Thomas Reo stood silhouetted against the church, shovelling the heap of earth back into the hole.

The Maori girls, whom Mrs Kemp trained in the house, had been busy. The table in the dining room was laid with scones and cakes and teacups. The fire burned in the grate. Mrs Kemp removed her bonnet and placed it on the hall table. She fussed over Mrs Clarke who had ridden over with her husband from the Waimate mission station, taking her bonnet and shawl and handing them to Mary Ann to place in the parlour.

'Now, come and have a cup of tea, Martha dear. You too Lizzie, you look frozen.'

Mr Kemp and Mr Clarke, friends since childhood, stood with their backs to the fire, cups of tea in their hands. Elizabeth crouched by the fender and stretched out her hands behind the black trousered legs. The men's voices murmured above her, discussing committee meetings and the people of the east coast.

Mr Clarke suddenly noticed Elizabeth. 'Hello, want to come and warm yourself?' He moved to let her in. 'Creep in round here. By the way, James, how's Henry getting on? Edward seems to be enjoying himself immensely at Norwich.'

The two ladies came close. 'Are you talking of our Henry?' asked Mrs Kemp.

'I was just asking how he was getting on.'

'He seems to be liking it and doing quite well. But I am worried about his health. My sister Ann says he gets a lot of coughs and colds. The climate does not seem to agree with him.'

'That's unfortunate. The Williamses are also a bit worried about their Edward. He seems homesick and quite depressed. They are even talking of bringing him back. At least our two boys are at the same school and know each other.' Mr Clarke put his cup back onto the saucer and turned to Mrs Kemp. 'I'm sorry about this little lad today, Charlotte; I didn't have time to say before.'

'Thank you, George, it has happened to you and now it has happened to us. I think we can thank the Lord that we have so many healthy children.' She looked down at Elizabeth. 'I'm afraid Lizzie will miss him the most after all the time she has spent looking after him for me. Time will hang on your hands, won't it, love?'

Elizabeth could sense their sympathetic eyes looking down at her. She looked at the fire.

Mrs Clarke broke the silence. 'Then how would it be if Elizabeth came and stayed with us for a few days? I'm sure we could find plenty for you to do, Lizzie. You could help me with my babies.'

'Well, Lizzie, you'd like that, wouldn't you?' asked her mother.

She sounded almost as though she was trying to hustle her away, thought Elizabeth, but she nodded. She did not mind the thought of going away from the settlement for a while. Sometimes she felt as though her whole life was, and would always be, enclosed within these few encircling hills.

'We'll have to leave soon, though,' said Mr Clarke. 'The rain is threatening. Can you get some things together quickly?'

'You mean, take her now?' asked Mrs Kemp.

'Why not?'

Mrs Kemp turned to Mrs Clarke. 'Oh, Martha, that's a bit sudden for you, isn't it?'

'Nonsense, we came over on two horses. She can ride back on Selim with you, can't she, George?'

It was soon arranged. They walked out to the cattle yard where the horses were tethered. Elizabeth was lifted up behind Mr Clarke. Her crutches and small bundle of clothes were tied onto the front of the saddle.

As they rode up the hill behind the house a few spots of rain began to fall. Elizabeth clung onto Mr Clarke and was partly protected by his cloak. It was very different to riding with her father who sat solid and immovable as a tree trunk. Mr Clarke, taller and thinner, was more like a branch that moved with the wind.

It was a monotonous journey over gently rising, fern-clad hills. The road was in good condition, having been recently widened and levelled to take the drays that carried goods between the settlements.

'What do you think of my road, Elizabeth?' asked Mr Clarke, in a proprietary tone.

'It's very nice,' said Elzabeth politely.

'But wait till you see my bridge.'

As they rose out of the hollow that contained Kerikeri and the Bay of Islands, the countryside suddenly stretched out all around them. Inlets, islands and sea lay behind. And in front was a crumpled mass of land. The volcanic hills of Pouerua, Te Ahuahu, Pokaka and others stood like pots on a table, many stepped and bristling with Maori fortifications. The clouds trailed ragged skirts of rain across the hilltops.

It was not far before the road started to descend again into the wide valley of the Waitangi River. From there the inland missionary settlement of Waimate was clearly visible on the opposite bank, a geometric pattern of fields and young hedges.

In the base of the valley, next to a group of shaggy huts, was Mr Clarke's bridge. Set across the meandering river, it looked solid, neat and alien. The huts were deserted, used only in the summer by the cultivators of the kumara plots along the river bottom. Plants new to the Maori, and grown from seed provided by the missionaries, were also in evidence where a patch of maize stalks waved their tattered remnants.

The horses trotted onto the bridge where they pranced and sidled, made uneasy by the hollow tones beneath their feet. Mr Clarke reined his horse to a stop so that Elizabeth could look about.

'It is a beautiful bridge,' she said.

'Sixty-seven feet!'

'Fancy!' Elizabeth hoped she sounded suitably impressed. In fact she had never seen anything like it and had nothing with which to compare it. It was a bit like a jetty that did not end in the sea but on another piece of land, and compared with the jetty at home it was certainly a solid structure.

'You must be very proud of it,' she ventured.

'Yes,' he admitted. 'Little did your father and I know what we were going to have to be when we came out here, Elizabeth. House builders, road makers, wheelwrights, farmers, even bridge builders. I don't think, however, that anything else has given me quite so much satisfaction.' He bent closer and whispered, 'I must confess to a secret sin, Elizabeth. I'm very proud of myself.'

'I won't tell anyone,' she assured him.

He gave a short chuckle and, wheeling the horse about, continued up the hill. They could see Mrs Clarke, well ahead of them by now.

This side of the valley rose steeply from the river to the ridge on which stood Waimate. Beside the road new ground was being broken in for farming. Heaps of stones, removed as the land was ploughed, lay around the perimeter, to be built into walls. Lengths of tough bracken roots had been piled into mounds to be burned when they dried out in the summer.

Mr Davis, who managed the mission farm, was guiding the horse and plough, working near the track. He pulled to a halt as they rode up.

'Nearly finished, Richard?' called Mr Clarke.

'Last turn.'

'Planting wheat here?'

'No, I'm trying potatoes first to break up the ground. I should be able to get them out before it's time to plant the wheat. I've put them down there already.'

Elizabeth followed his directing arm but could see nothing except the bare ridged earth, and the desolate heaps of stones and twisted black roots.

'Well, I'd better get finished before it rains. I'm cold enough as it is without getting wet too.' He flicked the reins and the horse strained forward.

The sky was certainly growing darker and the white buildings of the mission station glowed luminous against the thunderous background as they rode up the hill, spurring the horse forward to catch up with Mrs Clarke. A dovecote stood in front of the Clarkes' house and the bright white doves fluttered into the openings to gain shelter as the first heavy drops began to fall.

Mr Clarke lifted Elizabeth down from the horse and across to the verandah, then ran back for her crutches and bundle of clothes. Mrs Clarke was already there, holding onto her horse. Mr Clarke took her reins and, leaning against the rain, led the two horses over to the shed.

As they opened the front door a chorus of voices arose.

'Mama is back!'

Children seemed to gather from all directions. They emerged from doors, ran down stairs and slid down bannisters. The hall filled rapidly although, as Elizabeth later realized, there were only seven of them. The two oldest were at school and the baby in bed but, for a moment, it was quite overwhelming.

'Lizzie has come to stay,' announced Mrs Clarke.

'Goody,' said a small girl, grabbing her hand. 'Come and play with me.'

'Just a moment, Martha,' Mrs Clarke interrupted the daughter who shared her name. 'Give Lizzie time to take a breath. She will be sharing your room so you can take her things up.

I expect that she would like to get warm first. I know I would. Is the fire on in the parlour?'

'No, in the dining room, we've been in there.'

Elizabeth was led into a room where bright firelight shone between the babies' napkins, which decorated a brass fireguard. The floor was littered with toys, bricks, dolls, books and balls. In the middle of it all sat a small fat toddler, obviously wet, and bawling.

Mrs Clarke swept over and picked him up. 'Oh, for goodness' sake, Hopkins,' she said as she tucked him under her arm, his limbs flailing. The sudden movement seemed to deprive him of breath and sound. She whisked an aired napkin off the fireguard and departed through the kitchen door.

Elizabeth had barely got herself settled in a chair by the fire, with her crutches against the side, when Mrs Clarke reappeared with Hopkins still tucked under her arm. She came and plonked him onto Elizabeth's lap.

'He's dry now,' she announced. 'Keep him happy for a moment, dear.' She lifted the remaining napkins from the fender, and handed them to her daughter, Mary. 'Fold them up, dearest,' she ordered.

She turned to the rest of her untidy children 'William, put the blocks away if you have finished with them. Henry, the books belong in the bookcase.' Mrs Clarke picked up a ball. 'And you know you are not allowed to play with balls in the house.' She handed a rag doll to her daughter, Martha, after straightening its skirt. 'How about putting Polly to bed, dear. It's nearly time for tea.' In a few seconds chaos was turned to order. Used to her mother's gentle admonishments, Elizabeth watched with widening eyes.

It did not take Elizabeth long to realize that she, also, was being watched. Hopkins, deposited so suddenly on the knee of a complete stranger, sat staring at her with fixed intensity. Uncertain whether to relax or yell, he was hovering on the brink when Elizabeth noticed him.

'Hello,' she said. His mouth puckered at the corners. Elizabeth suddenly recollected Sam's delight at the toe game. '*This little piggy*,' she said hastily, wiggling his big toe, '*went to market. This little piggy stayed at home.*' Hopkins transferred his astonished gaze to his toes. By the time she had reached, '*This little piggy cried wee, wee, wee, all the way home,*' his fascination had overcome his fear. Elizabeth launched onto the other foot and, by the end of that, he was laughing happily.

'Good, I'm glad you're getting on so well,' said Mrs Clarke, picking up the pile of folded napkins. 'Tea won't be long, then I'll put him to bed. You don't mind keeping him amused, do you, dear?' She departed into the kichen with a backward call: 'Come and lay the table for tea, Martha, dear.'

In the days that followed Elizabeth and Hopkins became fast friends. He was delighted to have someone who played and didn't suddenly dart away on pursuits of her own. Elizabeth was happy to amuse him as she had Sam, with the added advantage that he did not need to be carried and could toddle along beside her clutching a handful of skirt.

In a few days the character of Sam seemed to have blended with that of Hopkins and Elizabeth had to admit, with almost a feeling of guilt, that it was difficult for her to recall the features of her little brother.

When Hopkins slept, Elizabeth had no lack of things to do. The whole house moved at the pace that Mrs Clarke set and she was always calling out:

'William, please watch James for me.'

'There are weeds in the carrot patch, Henry.'

'How about cleaning the silver, Elizabeth?'

'Martha and Mary, your beds are not made.'

Elizabeth only had time to think at night, as she lay in bed, beside the warm brick chimney that ran up through the room. Then she would think of home. Lying in the warm darkness, listening to the sleeping sounds of Martha and Mary, she could see it in her mind. Certainly it was not as elegant as the Clarkes'; there were no curving bannisters or silver coffee pots, but it was home and she longed to go back.

It happened sooner than she expected. One morning, when playing with Hopkins, she heard a voice calling, 'Whoa there.' and then the sound of horses' hooves coming to a halt at the door. She looked up. Was that her father's voice? She reached for her crutches and swung to the doorway.

'Papa,' she cried.

Her father descended from the dray, holding the reins in one hand. 'Hello, Lizzie. Ready to come home?'

Before she could reply she heard Mrs Clarke's quick step behind her. 'James, don't say you've come to fetch Elizabeth. Hopkins will be heart-broken.'

'I've come to bring you some coal.'

'Coal, for me?'

'No, not for you, for the forge,' he smiled. 'It gives a better heat than wood. But I will take Lizzie too, if you don't mind. Perhaps she could get her things together while I take the cart over to the forge.'

'You'll stay for some lunch, surely?'

'Thank you, Martha. Yes, that would be good. I'll have to wash out the cart and get a load of flour from the mill, so that should give Elizabeth enough time.'

'I'll get started,' said Elizabeth, turning to the stairs. Hopkins sat on the bottom step, in the bright square of light from the doorway. He looked as though he knew something was happening and he didn't quite like it. Elizabeth felt a twinge of guilt.

'I'll come back soon, Hoppy, I promise.'

After lunch and farewells, Elizabeth climbed up onto the dray beside her father. He urged the horse forward. The cart jolted down to the river, passing the new ground that Mr Davis had been breaking in. To Elizabeth's surprise, the previously desolate patch of ridged ground had suddenly, in these last few days, come alive. Along each furrow a line of yellow-green dots was pushing up through the black earth. She could barely understand the great tide of excitement that rushed through her. It had all looked so dead, so depressing and empty, and now there was this: ridges of light, bright green, bringing it to life.

'Nothing ever stops, does it?' Elizabeth said on impulse. 'Even when you think it should.'

'Well …' said her father slowly, 'I can't say it ever entered my head that it, whatever it is, should stop just for me. But if you mean life in general, no, it doesn't stop. We've just got to get on with it, whatever happens. But I'm worried, Elizabeth. I don't think your mother realizes this at the moment. That's why I came and fetched you. I think your mother needs you. I'm not quite sure what, but there is something wrong.'

'With Mama?'

'Yes, she hasn't seemed overly upset by Sam going the way he did, but she's not behaving right.'

'What do you mean? Not behaving right?'

'I don't really know. She doesn't seem to notice people properly; it's as though we were hardly there.'

'Well, what can I do?'

'I don't know that either,' he said. 'Just be there, I think. You were always close. Perhaps she will talk to you.'

They came to the bridge. 'Isn't it a good bridge?' said Elizabeth. It was a deliberate attempt to end a conversation that bewildered her.

'Aye, he'll tackle anything, that George. Roads, houses and now bridges. He's a remarkable lad.'

'So are you,' said Elizabeth defensively. She remembered Mr Clarke's secret sin. 'You're better,' she added, making him laugh.

At length they reached Kerikeri. Nobody came out to meet them. Her father lifted her down near the back door then led the dray away to be unloaded.

Elizabeth pushed the door open and went into the kitchen. Mrs Reo was rolling some pastry on the table while her mother sat, peeling apples, at the other end.

'Well, if it isn't Elizabeth back,' exclaimed Mrs Reo. Not getting any reply from Mrs Kemp, she leant towards her and said in a louder voice, 'It's Elizabeth!' as though she was explaining something to a blind person.

Her mother glanced up at Elizabeth.

'Oh, it's you,' she said, and went on peeling the apple in her hands.

CHAPTER 12

At last the stone store was almost completed. The stairs and shelves were finished, but the room was a mess. It had been partly used for storage for some time, with the stores stacked in heaps against the walls. They had been constantly moved as Mr Nisbet, the Scottish carpenter, tried to finish the woodwork. Wherever Mr Nisbet went with his hammer, the supplies parted like the Red Sea.

Now that the interior was finished, Mr Nisbet worked on the final glory, a clock tower. It had been decided to remove the clock from the church on the hill, where its weight threatened to crumble the plaster-and-lathe walls, and to place it in a small tower atop the store. Mr Nisbet sat astride the tower, nailing on the last of the wooden shingles.

Several people, adults and children, were scurrying back and forth between the new and old store, carrying boxes and bundles, like a colony of worker ants intent on moving their eggs to safety.

Elizabeth sat on an upturned box in the cool of the store, sorting nails into a set of cubicles that Mr Nisbet had built for them.

Away from the house and her mother, she felt more relaxed. Mrs Kemp's distant behaviour was upsetting for everyone.

Her father stood nearby, stacking the shelves with shirts, according to size. They worked in silence, intent on their sorting. The only sound was the tap-tap-tap of the hammer on the roof and the occasional pause and scuffle as Mr Nisbet placed another shingle, then tap-tap-tap again.

At one point there was a longer pause, then a longer scuffle as though Mr Nisbet was changing position, but this time the scuffling grew louder. Suddenly there was a wild cry, taken up by shrieks from the ground. Mr Kemp looked up, startled. Elizabeth paused and turned, nail in hand. 'What was that?'

A small, dark figure darted into the oblong of light that was the doorway. It was Sarah. 'Papa, Papa, Mr Nisbet has fallen off the roof!'

'Good God!' exclaimed Mr Kemp. Dropping his bundle of shirts, he rushed for the door. Elizabeth threw the nail in the cubicle, reached for her crutches and followed her father round the side of the building to where people were converging. Mr Nisbet lay on the ground, muttering and moaning. He was propped up on his elbows, his head stretched back in agony. He groaned, 'Damned hammer … flaming leg …'

Mr Kemp knelt down beside him. 'Thank God you're still alive, Ben. Where is the pain, man? What have you done?'

'Oh, 'tis my leg. No, 'tis my ankle. It could be my hip, oh…!' He leant over to one side, rubbing his hip and thigh.

'Don't move, Ben,' cautioned Mr Kemp, 'till we see that nothing is broken.'

Mr Nisbet fell back onto the ground.

'Sarah, run and get a cushion,' ordered her father, as he tried to ease up the trouser leg. It was obvious in an instant that the lower part of the leg and ankle were swelling rapidly.

'I'll have to take your boot off, Ben,' Mr Kemp told him. 'It may hurt. I'll be as careful as I can.' He untied the laces and loosened them as far as possible. Luckily the old boot slipped off easily with only one long groan from the patient. The sock was soon cut away, to expose the damaged foot.

'It's pretty swollen. It could be broken or it could be just a bad sprain. We'll hope for the latter. You say your hip hurts, too?'

'Yes, but it's easing off now. I must have just jarred it.'

'If so, you're the luckiest man I know.' Mr Kemp glanced up. 'It's all of twenty-four feet.'

'Damn it,' said Mr Nisbet, 'and only ten more shingles to go.'

Whether the leg was broken or not they never discovered. The injury was kept well splinted, but it took a number of weeks for the swelling to subside completely. After sitting for several days on the verandah, unoccupied, Mr Nisbet's temper began to fray.

'I can't sit here day after day,' he complained to Elizabeth.

'You could borrow my crutches,' she offered.

'Better still, I could make my own.'

His request for timber and tools was soon fulfilled and he proceeded to make a pair for himself, like Elizabeth's, only longer. He started to shuffle about and eventually got back to the store where he spent his time sitting on a box, planing and dressing pieces of wood ready for use.

One day Elizabeth pulled herself up the stone store steps and peered inside. 'I've brought you some lunch,' she called.

Mr Nisbet put down his tools. 'Keep it there, lass,' he said.

'I'll come out in the sunshine.' He reached for his crutches and limped out to the door. He eased himself down onto the step beside her.

'We're a gammy pair with our crutches,' he chuckled.

Elizabeth didn't answer, but handed him the lunch, packed in a little flax basket.

'Tell me,' he continued, 'does your leg pain you, like mine, that you cannot walk on it?'

'No,' she snapped. 'And it's not worth talking about, thank you.'

'Now, now,' he replied, 'it's no good getting like that about it.'

'I'm not getting like anything,' said Elizabeth. 'I just don't like talking about it, if you don't mind.'

'Why not?'

'I just don't want to,' she answered angrily, fully aware that she was being impertinent to an adult, and flushing in consequence.

Mr Nisbet busied himself with his bread and cheese.

Elizabeth looked away towards the pa, blinking.

''Tis not just idle curiosity,' he said. 'I had a purpose in asking. I thought I might be able to help.'

Elizabeth turned back to look at him. 'Help? In what way?'

'Well, I've found out how awkward it is with these damned crutches.'

'It is,' she agreed.

'And I got to thinking. Why do you have to use them?'

'I have too. My leg just crumples up.'

'But it doesn't hurt?'

'Not now.'

'Then all it needs, like mine, is a splint to stiffen it.'

'But I don't think I could move my hip forward.'

'Deary me, couldn't you swing it forward?'

'I don't know.'

'Well, don't you think, if I make you a splint, it's worth a try?'

Elizabeth nodded.

'Good. You can't just pretend things aren't there, when they are. Think, if it works you may be able to walk without those crutches.'

'I could even carry things,' said Elizabeth, eager in spite of herself.

'Right then, that's settled. Tomorrow, bring some strips of rag for tying it onto your leg.'

True to his word, Mr Nisbet worked on the splint all the next morning. By the time Elizabeth brought his lunch, it was made.

'Did you bring the rags?' he asked.

'Yes.'

'Come and sit on this box then.'

They proceeded, between them, to bind her leg to the splint which Mr Nisbet had made with a right-angled foot support. Elizabeth smiled at the way her leg stuck out at such a funny angle to the seat.

'Right then, stand you up,' he ordered, pulling her to her feet. But when she straightened her good leg, the weight of the wood tipped her sideways. Mr Nisbet grabbed her before she fell.

'Steady lass, steady,' he muttered, looking down. 'Well now, without use, it seems that your bad leg has not grown at the same pace as the other.'

'I knew it wouldn't work,' said Elizabeth.

'Not so fast,' he grumbled. 'Who said it wouldn't work? You're like a wobbly table. All we have to do is level you off a bit.'

'Chop a bit off the good one?'

'No lass, add a bit to the other. Now, hang onto the back of the chair. Stand up straight, shoulders back, that's it. I'll measure the difference.' Mr Nisbet sat on the box beside her with the measuring stick in his hand, leaning forward to peer at the markings.

'Right, one and a quarter,' he muttered. 'Take it off while I cut a bit of wood.'

Elizabeth unwrapped the strips and gave him the splint, then sat rolling up the rags as he nailed the block of wood onto the base of the splint.

'Now, try again,' Mr Nisbet ordered.

This time she was able to stand, but when she tried to swing her leg forward the wood scraped on the floor.

'Oh, it's hopeless,' exclaimed Elizabeth. 'I'll never be any better.'

'Then you'll not be any worse, will you? And you'll continue to muddle through.'

'What do you mean, muddle through?' laughed Elizabeth.

'That's what we all do, lassie, muddle through. You can make great plans, but something, or someone, is bound to upset them. So we go on muddling, and hope for the best. But it's not hopeless in this case. All we need is a wee bit of clearance. Now, sit down and I'll try to plane a bit off the bottom.'

They proceeded by dint of trial and error to fashion a splint that supported her leg, yet swung a fraction above the floor when she twisted her hip forward. With each step of progress

Elizabeth began to hope. At first timidly, then confidently, and finally she said, 'It will work, Mr Nisbet. I know it will if I practise.'

'That's the girl, Lizzie. Now I told you, didn't I?'

Elizabeth continued to practise, lurching around the store, clinging to anything that came to hand — chairs, boxes, tables or shelves.

'Now try walking across the floor to me,' urged Mr Nisbet.

Elizabeth pushed herself away from the chair she was holding and turned to face him. Without the crutches, she held her arms out for balance. Then, standing resolutely on her one good leg, she slung the whole side of her body forward, swinging the splinted leg across the floor. Then, balancing on it carefully, she shunted her sound leg forward.

'That's the idea, lassie,' said Mr Nisbet. 'Again, lass; you're doing famously.'

Elizabeth repeated the exercise.

'That's it, that's it,' he urged, with each clumsy step. Slowly she crossed the open floor until she reached him. 'You did it, lass,' he chortled. 'Now there'll be no stopping you.'

'Let's go and show Papa. He's just round the back in the smithy. Come with me and we'll show him.' Elizabeth grabbed Mr Nisbet's hand as though to pull him up.

'Alright, lass, give me time to find my flaming crutches.' He felt about behind his chair. 'You'll need yours, too. You're not up to walking that far yet.'

Together, they limped round to the smithy. Mr Kemp stood by the glowing forge, beating out a horseshoe. As they neared he plunged it into a barrel of water and the steam rose in a hissing cloud.

'Please, Papa, I've got something to show you,' called Elizabeth.

Mr Kemp put the horseshoe down and turned.

Ten yards away, Elizabeth felt her face flush. 'Now, just stand there and watch,' she ordered.

Elizabeth dropped her crutches to the ground, hesitated for a second then lurched forward with a few ungainly steps. 'See, I can walk,' she shouted. 'Did you see me?'

Mr Kemp looked astounded for a moment then he stepped forward. Elizabeth lifted her skirt to show him the splint.

'See, it was Mr Nisbet's idea. Isn't he clever?'

Her father seemed to have difficulty finding his voice. 'Indeed he is,' he said finally.

'Don't tell Mama,' said Elizabeth urgently. 'I want to surprise her myself. After I've practised.'

Elizabeth found that the best time to practise was early in the morning, when her mother was getting dressed upstairs. At that hour, no one was about, and she could be on the front verandah alone, walking up and down close to the rail which she could use to steady herself. She had taken Richard into her confidence and was able to keep the splint and the cloth strips in his little bedroom that opened off the side of the porch. He was delighted to be entrusted with the secret.

One day a short time later, while putting the splint away after a practice, Elizabeth heard the front door open. Looking round the porch door, she saw that it was her father. She nearly called out to him and then saw that her mother was close behind. Not wanting her to see the splint, she kept quiet. Her mother seemed to be pleading with her husband.

'James, James, do you have to go?'

Elizabeth withdrew her head abruptly. She heard her father's appeasing voice.

'Of course I have to go, Charlotte, you know that.'

'Couldn't one of the others?'

'But it's my turn. Edmonds went last week.'

'Please James. I'm frightened.'

'But why? There's nothing to be frightened of. The other men are here if you need them.'

'It's … it's … oh, please.'

'Now come on, love, stop being ridiculous.' An irritated note was creeping into his voice. 'I'm only going to Taronui. I'll be back tonight or, at worst, first thing in the morning.'

Elizabeth heard her mother's voice, low and pleading..

'I can't. Oh don't … Please, James.'

'Charlotte, dear, can't you tell me what is wrong?' asked her father.

'Not really. No.'

'Then I have no real reason to stay, have I?'

'I don't know,' said her mother, in a small, sad voice.

'Then I'll be back tonight,' said her father, a trifle testily. 'Now, please try to pull yourself together, Charlotte.' Turning abruptly, he picked up his bag and strode down the path.

A few seconds' silence followed and Elizabeth suddenly realized that her mother had moved along the verandah towards her and was sitting in the old armchair that stood by the door. She could hear the words that she was murmuring to herself.

'I've had enough, I've had enough. Oh, God, I've had enough.' Then Mrs Kemp got up and went back inside.

Elizabeth sat pondering the interchange. What was her mother frightened of? Elizabeth could not think of anything.

Besides, her mother was not usually a timorous person.

In the kitchen she found Hana and Sarah Waiapu making bread.

'Where's Mama?' asked Elizabeth.

'She said she had a headache and went to her room,' said Hana.

'She asked to be left alone,' added Sarah.

A hush possessed the house for the rest of the day. As it was not a school day, neither the Maori girls nor the children knew what they should be doing.

Mary Ann took a tray up at lunchtime, and again at tea-time.

'How is she?' Elizabeth asked.

'I don't know. She is just sitting on a chair looking out of the window. I told her I had brought the tray and she said, 'Put it over there.' Mary Ann shrugged. 'She didn't say any more.'

CHAPTER 13

Elizabeth awoke with a jerk. A wedge of moonlight slanted through the window. She wondered what had woken her so suddenly and lay still, listening. The only sounds were a distant morepork, and the nearby river tumbling over the rocks.

Then she heard it again: a shuffle followed by a grinding sound, so close that she realized it was in the house. Even upstairs? She got out of bed and stood shivering on the cold floor. The moon gave enough light for her to find her crutch and limp to the door. She opened it cautiously. She waited and the noise came again, from her parents' room. There was a thin thread of light under the door. Elizabeth went across and knocked, pressing her ear to the wood. There was silence for a moment, then her mother's voice.

'Who is it?'

'It's me, Lizzie.'

'Come on in, quickly.'

Elizabeth opened the door and slid in.

'Shut it now,' ordered her mother.

Inside the room, Elizabeth looked around. The light came

from a single candle by the bed. Her mother was leaning against a large chest of drawers. She was in her nightdress, her hair hanging over one shoulder in a long plait. She looked exhausted.

The chest had been pulled out, about two feet away from the wall. Several reasons for this strange act flashed through Elizabeth's mind: a rat perhaps, or something fallen behind?

'What has happened?' she asked, but her mother ignored the question.

'Quick, help me,' she said. 'You get that end and we'll rock it out.'

Elizabeth leant her crutch against the wall and hopped to the end of the chest. Gripping either side of it, she balanced on her good leg. 'How far out do you want it?' she asked.

'Against the door.'

A chill of fear ran through Elizabeth's chest and up into her throat. 'What for?'

Again her mother ignored her question. 'You lift your end first then I'll lift mine,' she ordered.

Elizabeth pressed her shoulder against the chest and tried to grip it and lift. 'I can't, Mama. It's too heavy.'

Her mother looked distraught. 'Oh, what are we going to do?' she wailed, glancing furtively at the back window of the narrow room.

Suddenly she darted across to it, pulled the lace curtain aside, and peered out.

'They're coming,' she cried. 'I can see them in the shadows. Look.' She pointed to the window and Elizabeth went over and looked out. Who did her mother think she'd seen?

The moon, surrounded by a bluish haze, appeared fitfully between the moving clouds. It was easy to imagine people moving in the shadows it cast, but she could see nothing definite. 'There's nobody. Who can you see?' she asked.

'You know that Hongi has died.' It was an accusation not a question.

'Yes,' faltered Elizabeth.

'Well, they will be coming. They always do.'

Suddenly her mother wheeled round to face her and pointed at the cradle in the corner. Empty, since Sam had died. 'And stop that child crying,' she ordered.

The chill struck Elizabeth again but this time it stayed like a cold sickness in her stomach. Her mother was out of her mind! Elizabeth stood rigid, staring.

'Hurry,' urged her mother. 'Keep him quiet.'

Elizabeth limped over and sat on the stool beside the cradle. She started to rock it backwards and forwards, a confusion of thoughts running through her mind. Did her mother think Sam was still alive? Why was she talking about Hongi? He had died years ago. She could vaguely remember the tumult of that time. The fear that they would be attacked by other tribes, now that their protector was gone. Elizabeth could just recall how she and the other children had been sent over to Paihia. Valuables had been hidden under floorboards or buried in the garden. Daily the missionaries had expected raiding parties to descend and strip them of their possessions, or even kill them. Had her mother's mind slipped back all those years?

What could she do? Fetch help? John and Mere would be the nearest. It would mean going out among those moonlit shadows. The thought filled her with terror. She half believed that they were there, those scurrying figures of her mother's imagination.

If only her father were here.

As if reading her thoughts her mother asked, 'Where is James?'

'He's gone to Taronui.'

'Always away when I want him,' she said peevishly.

'Don't you remember, he went this morning. Don't you remember?' pleaded Elizabeth. 'He said he might be back tonight. He might come.' She hoped desperately that he had not decided to stay.

But her mother was not listening. She was still crouched under the window, peering between the curtains.

Time crept on, the candle melting lower and lower. Her mother dragged the chest, inch by inch, across the floor. Elizabeth was relieved to realize that it would be a long slow job. Apart from her mother's lack of strength, the windows distracted her. She kept rushing from one to the other, then back to the chest. Elizabeth continued to rock the cradle, gazing into its empty, dark interior.

'Father, please come home.' She sent up a silent prayer. Not to the God whom she used to talk to. He seemed more unreal than ever, a vanishing star, soon to dissolve completely. No, this was a plea from mind to mind, to her father.

Her mother was still by the window, twitching the curtains. Suddenly she let out a cry and rushed back to the chest of drawers. 'They're here. I saw their light coming up the river. I knew they'd come.' She leant heavily against the chest and tried to push it.

Elizabeth hopped to the window. There *was* a light coming up the inlet. In a brief patch of moonlight she caught sight of a bellying sail. It was no native canoe. 'Mama, don't worry, it's Father.'

Her mother took no notice, still intent on moving the chest.

'Mama, stop doing that,' Elizabeth insisted. 'Papa will be home in a moment. Come and see, he's coming up to the jetty now.'

'It's them, I knew they'd come,' insisted her mother, hysteria in her voice.

Elizabeth watched the boat drawing up to the jetty. After a few moments a light moved towards the gate, flick, flick, flick through the gaps in the fence. Then the gate opened.

Elizabeth lifted the window and leant out. 'Papa, come quickly,' she called. 'Please!'

Suddenly, she felt herself grabbed from behind and flung to the floor. Her mother's hand was clasped roughly over her mouth.

'Hush you silly child, they'll hear you!'

Elizabeth lay still. She didn't want to fight her mother. Besides, she could hear her father's footsteps crunching on the gravel path, the front door opening and his heavy boots thumping up the stairs. The door was pushed open and crashed against the chest of drawers, now only about a foot from the door. His head appeared round the door and he seemed to take in the situation at a glance. He squeezed through the narrow opening and rushed over to take hold of his wife.

'Charlotte, dear, what are you doing?' He helped her to stand and she looked at him as if dazed.

'Oh, James, it's you. This silly girl was calling to them.'

'Who?' asked Mr Kemp. 'Elizabeth was calling to me. There's no one else out there.'

Elizabeth was sitting up by now, sobbing against the wall beneath the window. 'She thinks Hongi has just died. That they are coming to raid us,' she said between sobs and shuddering sniffs. 'She's mad!'

'Oh no, Charlotte, not that,' he whispered.

His wife leant against him, oblivious of Elizabeth's outcry, plucking at the buttons on his waistcoat. 'Why are you never here when I want you?' she asked pettishly.

Mr Kemp was silent for a moment. 'I'm sorry,' he said eventually. Then, turning her about, he led her over to the bed. 'You can go to bed now, love, I'll look after everything.' He helped her get in, then sat on a chair beside the bed. Mrs Kemp lay back on the pillow and closed her eyes, still clasping his hand. He bowed his head right down to the clasped hands and sat unmoving, his great hunched, despairing shadow looming over the room. At length Elizabeth's stifled sobs made him look up.

'Do you want to go back to bed, Lizzie, love?' he said gently. 'You've had a bad night.'

She wiped her sleeve across her face. 'No, please, Papa. I don't want to go back to my room on my own. Let me stay.'

'Do you want my handkerchief?'

Elizabeth groped for her crutch then pulled herself up. She took the handkerchief and blew her nose.

'I know what I could do with,' her father said. 'Something hot. A cup of tea or some soup. Do you think you could stir up the fire and get me some? It was a rough, cold trip. I shouldn't really have made it at night and it took longer than I thought it would. But I'm glad I did.'

'Yes, but I don't think there is any soup left.'

'Tea will do. I don't want to leave your mother just yet.'

'No, but I can't carry it upstairs.'

'I'll just wait until she's right off to sleep. I'll come down when I'm sure. Take the candle if you want it.'

'I'll see by the light in the hall.'

'And a bit of bread and butter,' he called after her, as she edged out of the door.

There was still a slight red glow among the embers of the kitchen fire. Elizabeth scattered wood shavings onto the ashes, gave it a few puffs from the leather bellows and in a few seconds a bright curl of flame crept up the edge of a shaving and leapt onwards. Several quickly placed sticks of kindling soon caught, sending the light flaring across the wooden slab walls of the kitchen. Elizabeth lit the candle from the flames.

Soon the fire was blazing. The kettle stood on the hob and Elizabeth lifted it over to the hook above the flames. Strangely, it still felt warm and she glanced across at the kitchen clock. It was only five past ten; she had thought it well past midnight.

She busied herself, getting china out and putting tea in the pot, trying to forget what had happened. But her mind was in turmoil, and she felt chilled despite the fire. Why was her mother losing her mind? Was it Elizabeth's fault? Perhaps she could have done better at looking after the younger children. But, worse, what if her outburst after Sam's death had upset her mother to such an extent that it had provoked this disaster?

By the time she heard her father descending the stairs, the tea was made and the bread buttered. He came across and leant against the chimneypiece, staring into the fire.

'This is a bad business, Lizzie,' he said finally.

Elizabeth didn't know what to say or how to talk about her guilt. She picked up the teapot and poured the tea. 'I'm glad you came home,' she said at length. 'I don't know what I would have done.'

'I'm sorry, love, it's my fault. I shouldn't have gone away this morning. I should have stayed when she asked me to.'

'Oh no, Papa, it's my fault. I'm always upsetting Mama. And when Sam died I got angry and said some awful things. Awful …' Tears escaped and trickled down her nose.

'Here, don't cry,' he said, sitting down on the chair to meet her eyes. He handed her his handkerchief once more. 'It's nobody's fault and everybody's fault. None of us saw what was happening. If there's any blame, it's mine for bringing her here. It's the committee's for threatening to move us. It's all you children for just being … well, children. But you can't help making mistakes; we all do. And it all got too much for her. We should have noticed, particularly I should have, and I didn't. What matters now is that we get her better, so dry up your tears. Perhaps it's just the strain of it all and after a good night's sleep she may wake up quite all right. And it will all be over.'

'But what if she isn't?' Elizabeth said. 'What about the others? Sarah and William are so little. What can we say to them?' She suddenly wanted to cover up this terrible person, shut her in her room upstairs. Hide her!

'All we can say is that she is not well and needs to rest. That is the truth,' said her Father calmly. He looked into his cup, warming his hands around it. 'And we must pray.'

'As if that would do any good,' said Elizabeth, in a bitter voice.

Her father looked up. 'What?'

Elizabeth placed both hands on the table and leant forward, on the edge of tears. 'I said, that won't do any good.'

'Elizabeth?'

'Papa, I have prayed and prayed for my leg to get better. I

prayed about Sam, too. And what good did that do? And now, look at Mama. After all she's done for God.' She finished off with a sob of anguish. 'He doesn't care, he doesn't care at all. I don't even think there is such a person!' she ended defiantly, her words falling through the silence.

'No,' agreed her father after a pause. 'There isn't such a person.'

Elizabeth looked at him in amazement. 'Papa?'

'Because he's not a person like us, not a person to be bargained with.'

'Well, what is he?'

'You've heard it often enough. "God is love." Then our prayers must be for love, in us, so that we can help your mother. Do you understand that?'

Elizabeth shook her head. 'I don't know, I don't think so,' she said wearily. 'No, I don't understand at all.' She was trembling, though it wasn't cold beside the fire. 'I don't understand hundreds of things.'

Mr Kemp reached out and drew her onto his knee. He put his arms around her and in despair she turned her head into his coat. He rocked her gently.

'Poor Lizzie,' he muttered into her hair. 'You've got enough to bear. I don't understand hundreds of things either.'

Elizabeth rubbed her face against the rough black material of his coat. She could feel his strong blacksmith's arms about her and his cheek resting on the top of her head.

'Papa, if you don't understand either, what are we here for?'

Mr Kemp didn't answer for a moment. Then he spoke slowly. 'Do you think I don't ask myself that sometimes?' He paused again. Elizabeth could sense that he was trying to think what to say so she sat still, leaning against his chest and looking at the flames sinking back into the logs as they burnt out. Finally he said, 'The Maoris we know here are our friends now and, hopefully, the little bit I do understand is important to them. I know I thought differently when we first came. And probably they only wanted us then for what they could get from us. But we have both changed and we can't leave them now. We can't leave them to their own wars of revenge nor, though I hate to say it, to our own countrymen — many of whom only come here to plunder and degrade them, and they're going to keep coming. We've got to help them over that hurdle. And we have to show them that we have some good to offer as well. Love and forgiveness, they're the only strengths they'll have soon. And we may be the only people who will stand up for them. I don't know, but I sadly fear it. And I know your mother thinks this too despite … despite everything.' He paused. 'Does that help?'

'I think so,' she whispered, wondering whether it did.

They sat in silence, looking at the sinking fire.

'It's time you were in bed, Lizzie,' said her father at length. 'And I had better go and see your mother again.'

Elizabeth leant against him, making no effort to move. She did not want to break the feeling of strength and safety and love that he gave her. And she couldn't help hearing the text that William had learnt. It kept repeating in her head. 'God is love, and he that dwelleth in love dwelleth in God, and God in him.'

CHAPTER 14

November 1835

Dear Henry,

I have been waiting for news of a boat going back to England, to tell you the awful news about Mama. She is ill. She seems to have lost her mind. Or so it was when I left Kerikeri. William and I are at Waimate. Messages do come to us from Father and he says that she is getting better slowly. I hope that is so, because she seemed very unhappy when we left, with her mind constantly switching direction. Father tells us that she spends many hours in deep sleep which he feels will lead to her mind at length being restored.

Because of this Papa has told the Church committee that he wishes to resign. He also asked, if they are intending to close the mission at Kerikeri, that he be able to rent the house. I think that he is right to do this. Seeing Mother as she is now, we could not move her. There is one gleam of hope. The committee in England is against the closure and has suggested that one missioner remain. Let us hope and pray that they choose Papa.

The family has all been sent to different places: James and Richard are still attending school at Paihia and staying with the Williamses at weekends. Mary Ann and Sarah have stayed at Kerikeri, but under the care of Mrs Edmonds. As I told you, William and I are at Waimate, with the Clarkes, where we have been for almost three months now.

I'm sorry, but there is even more sad news. You probably remember my telling you that John and Mere Taua had gone up to Whangaroa to do missionary work there. Mr Clarke also goes there once a month to see that all is going well. He tells me that John is very sick and he fears that he may not be with us long. He appears to have all the symptoms of Consumption, from which so many Maori seem to suffer and die. I know just how attached you were to John and Mere, as they were to you. Mr Clarke also tells me that despite John's illness, they refuse to return to the comfort of Kerikeri, and continue on with their work at Whangaroa. They are very special people.

Christmas will be here in about a month. I expect we shall still be in Waimate. Everybody is very kind, but I wish we could all be back together again, with you back here, with Mama well again, and with John and Mere in Kerikeri — with everything just as it was. But I know that I am dreaming and it never will be. Everything changes.

I try to look after William as best I can. And with so many Clarkes to play with, he isn't being any trouble. I spend much time with Hopkins Clarke; he is a dear little boy and I can keep him amused as I did for Sam. It relieves the pressures on Mrs Clarke.

I remember, in my last letter, telling you about the splint that Mr Nisbet made for my leg. I continue to practise with it and can walk small distances, particularly indoors. Outside, it is awkward, as it catches on stones and tufts of grass. Also it is heavy, and I get tired. Mr Nesbit and Papa, I know, are trying to make a lighter one for me. I hesitate to tell them that I am not optimistic about its long-term use. They have worked so hard at it for my benefit. Perhaps I will be able to use it about the house and afford them some satisfaction.

It is spring here. In case you forget, we are the wrong way round. You may be in the autumn season, but here the primroses are flowering in the garden!

Your loving sister,
Elizabeth.

Dear Lizzie,

It seems ages since I saw you. Hemi says he is going over to Waimate tomorrow so I thought I would write to you. Write to me sometime, will you? Mrs Edmond is nice and I try to help her and look after Sarah but it is very boring with no school for us older girls.

It's getting warmer now, isn't it? I got out my summer dresses the other day and let out some of the tucks so they look all stripey and horrible, but I had to as I hadn't noticed how much I had grown.

I go and talk to Papa when he is working in the store; he says Mama is getting better slowly. He took me over to see her one day. She looked alright but thinner. She just said 'Hello Mary Ann,' then sat looking down the river. She didn't speak except when I asked her questions so it was very hard to talk to her. But, just as I was leaving she caught sight of my silly old pink shoes and she smiled and said, 'You've still got your elegant shoes.' Papa was so excited. As we walked back to the store he said it was the first time she had smiled for months. He even said, 'We'll have to put those shoes in a glass case,' but I think that's going a bit far, don't you?

You can have no idea what Mr Nisbet has built for us — it is called a shower-bath. He said he had seen them in Britain. Instead of sitting in the bath, we stand up and have water coming down on top of us. It is fun; Sarah and I go in together but we have to wash quickly before the water runs out. He has built it next to the wash house so that we can fill up a tank with warm water and it comes through a pipe in the wall and has a watering can thing on the end and it empties all over us. It is like being in a warm waterfall. Papa sometimes has just cold water but I don't fancy that.

Mr Nisbet is going away soon, now that the store is finished.

Please write to me; I like getting letters. Papa says we can come over to Waimate at Christmas for a party, won't that be fun?

With lots of love from your sister,
Mary Ann.

CHAPTER 15

It was the day of the Christmas party for the children of the missions and they, with their mothers, were all assembled in the front parlour of the Clarkes' home at Waimate. Elizabeth and William were still staying there and, though their brothers and sisters had been brought over by the Edmonds for the party — their mother had not come. Elizabeth was very disappointed, as she had heard such good reports of her improvement lately.

The door opened and in came Reverend Henry Williams, the senior missionary, who generally resided at Paihia. He was accompanied by a gentleman stranger. There was a pause in the hubbub and all the children turned to look at them. The two men surveyed the many eyes with slight embarrassment, before Mr Williams addressed his wife.

'My dear, this is Mr Charles Darwin, naturalist to *The Beagle*, Captain Fitzroy's ship. They are in port.'

Mrs Williams held out her hand and laughed breathlessly. 'I'm afraid you find us at a disadvantage, Mr Darwin, but it is the children's Christmas party. Please join us.'

'Enchanted, ma'am. It isn't often that I get invited to a party.'

'I think it is time for a pause, anyway. We've been playing games until I'm quite exhausted. Right children, I know Mrs Clarke has the feast prepared. To the kitchen,' she ordered. 'We will eat!'

There was a scramble for the door. Elizabeth was left sitting on a chair. Some of the adults, still talking, stood by the door.

'Come along, Elizabeth,' said Mr Clarke. 'You're not going to stay out here. You escort Mr Darwin through. We must go and help Martha with the ravenous hordes.'

Elizabeth brushed down her dress and stood up. She smiled shyly at the strange young man. He looked back with sharp, dark eyes under bristling brows. They stood for a moment in silence.

'Are you having a pleasant voyage?' she asked, having heard her mother ask that of visitors.

Mr Darwin smiled but answered equally politely. 'A very interesting voyage, perhaps more interesting than pleasant, I should say. I find a great deal of scope for my work.'

'What is a naturalist?' said Elizabeth.

'A naturalist studies animals, plants, rocks, hills. Anything that is natural, that is. Anything of nature, I should say.'

'You must be very busy.'

'Indeed,' agreed Mr Darwin.

Walking carefully on her splint, Elizabeth led him through the hall and the dining room to the kitchen, where two large tables, placed end to end, were surrounded by children.

'I must say that I have never seen a happier assemblage since I left England,' said Mr Darwin. 'Nor such a large collection of children.'

'Yes, there are rather a lot of us,' agreed Elizabeth. 'But we don't all live at Waimate. I'm from Kerikeri, so are the Edmonds and the Shepherds. We're going back tomorrow, I hope.'

Mrs Clarke bustled up. 'Now sit down here, Elizabeth, we've saved a place for you.'

What a feast they had. Sandwiches of ham, egg or cucumber. Then meat and chicken with salads. Followed by sponges and pastries. There were several large jugs of orange juice. And to finish, strawberries, fresh from the garden, with whipped cream.

Mr Darwin and Mr Williams stood behind Elizabeth's chair.

'I think that is the best meal I have had for four years,' exclaimed Mr Darwin, licking the cream from his fingers. 'Quite a change, I assure you, from ship's biscuits and salted meat. And is it all grown here?'

'Yes, we are extremely fortunate. Anything and everything seems to grow here,' agreed Mr Williams. 'We can show you round the gardens tomorrow. What else had you in mind to do?'

Mr Darwin expressed a wish to visit some local kauri trees, explaining that he had been told there were quite a few hereabout, there being none left near to the coast. Mr Williams agreed to take him there in the morning after attending a local committee meeting

Mr Darwin then suggested that he might arrange a game for the children in the morning. 'I see there are several small patches of native bush nearby,' he explained. 'How would it be if I offered a small prize for the best collection of native plants? Just a spray of leaves, with a fruit or flower if available.'

His proposal was agreed upon and next morning the children

gathered on the verandah to hear the rules and be sent on their way.

Elizabeth was left. She looked up shyly. 'I hope you don't mind if I don't go. I couldn't keep up,' she explained.

'Perhaps you could show me about?' suggested Mr Darwin. 'I should like very much to see the gardens.'

Elizabeth led him between the neat beds of vegetables and fruits. He seemed to get very excited when he saw the trusses of tomatoes and the size of the lettuces and cabbages.

'I think I can honestly say, Elizabeth, that in all my travels I have never seen so many plants growing in such abundance. And so many kinds,' he said. 'It must be a magnificent growing climate. Imagine! turnips and oranges together; and cabbages and cucumbers. They would hardly believe it back in England.'

Elizabeth could see nothing remarkable in this collection, so kept quiet. Mr Darwin, however, had suddenly become very much alive and talkative. He darted about, peering under leaves. He picked off a caterpillar and watched it crawl over his hand. He bent and pulled several weeds from a patch of carrots and waved them towards Elizabeth.

'Tut, tut,' he muttered, shaking his head. 'You'll have to be careful. Gorse!'

Elizabeth felt almost guilty. 'It's from the hedge,' she said.

'Yes, I noticed. Could be a problem in this climate. I saw a patch of wild leeks over there; they looked far too happy. It's very dangerous, you know, to remove things from their native habitat. Very dangerous — plants or animals.'

'Is it?'

'Yes, and we are the most dangerous of all. Remember that,

Elizabeth. But I must admit I am tremendously impressed. It's all very like England, isn't it? Even oaks,' he remarked, stopping beside a bed of striking acorns. 'Imagine when these grow big, it will be just like England, won't it?' He waved his arm at the fields and hedges.

'I don't know, I've never been there.'

Mr Darwin stopped and looked at her. 'Good gracious! No, I don't suppose you have.'

'Mama and Papa came from Norfolk,' said Elizabeth.

'Indeed! Lovely part of the country. I went to university not far from Norfolk, at a place called Cambridge.'

'My brother, Henry, wrote about a visit there to see a professor of languages.'

'I went there to study to be a minister in the church,' said Mr Darwin with a rueful shake of his head. 'Who knows, perhaps I might have become a missionary in New Zealand.'

'Why did you become a naturalist instead?' Elizabeth enquired.

'Alas! Beetles led me astray.'

'Beetles?'

'Yes, I discovered the world of beetles — thousands of them. The good Lord must have been inordinately fond of beetles. Do you know, Elizabeth, there appear to be more varieties of beetle on this earth than of any other animal?'

'Truly?' She pondered a moment. 'I can't say that I've seen all that many here.'

He gave a cursory glance about him. 'Well, neither have I, as yet — but they are no doubt here, hiding. In their thousands. All around us.'

'Hiding?' Elizabeth, looked about nervously.

'Yes, hiding: burrowing in the earth, crawling under rocks, chewing on leaves, crouching in the clefts of bark. I have seen beetles diving in the depths of ponds, flying through the air, and once,' he paused dramatically, 'I saw some swimming in the sea, six miles from land. Is that not astounding?'

Elizabeth nodded her head in agreement, but Mr Darwin was not to be stopped.

'Then,' he continued, 'in one day, in a country called Brazil, I discovered sixty-eight new species of beetle. In one day! How many would I have discovered in a week?' He stood gazing up at the sky. 'And how many more are there?'

Elizabeth could not decide whether he was addressing her or talking to himself – or even interrogating God. She decided to keep quiet.

Eventually he turned back to face her and in a lighter, bantering tone said, 'And do you think, Elizabeth, that the good Lord cares less for them than he does for us few mortals?'

Before she could reply, and indeed she did not know what to reply, a sullen William appeared through the gate, kicking a stone along the path. She was glad to change the subject.

'William, why aren't you collecting plants for Mr Darwin?'

''Cause William Clarke pinched some of mine, that's why. I'm not playing.'

Luckily a fantail chose that moment to come flitting into the garden. Mr Darwin swung round, following it with his eyes.

'What a remarkable bird,' he exclaimed.

The fantail obliged by skirting around him, swooping past his face, perching for a second on a nearby twig then spiralling up into the air, after an insect. At each movement of the bird, Mr Darwin followed. Together they turned about the garden, as though engaged in a solemn, twisting dance. He talked the whole time.

'Do you note how he moves? To catch insects, I see. And how he has adapted his tail to change direction in mid air?'

The fantail, finished with his investigation, rose suddenly and flew over the hedge. Mr Darwin stood, gazing after it. 'Remarkable tail! Eh, William?'

'It's a fantail,' explained William.

Mr Darwin smiled. 'And a very suitable name. The movement of its tail helps it to alter direction rapidly. It appears that over the centuries he has altered his tail to become a perfect aerial acrobat, in order to catch flies. D'you see?'

'No,' said William.

Mr Darwin sat down on a convenient wooden bench, placed there for a view across the valley. 'I'm not sure that I see, myself,' he said.

'But birds don't alter, they stay the same,' said Elizabeth.

'Yes, well they appear to,' said Mr Darwin, half to himself. 'Though, you know, I saw a great puzzle on our voyage over here. We called in at a group of islands — the Galapagos — on the way. There were some finches there, quite ordinary little birds, but the strange thing was that on each island of the group they had differently shaped beaks. They seemed to have altered them to suit the food supply available. Now how do you account for that?'

He gazed out over the valley, suddenly abstracted. 'Yes, how do you account for that?' he repeated.

'Perhaps,' said William, 'after God made them he saw they were having difficulties getting enough to eat with their beaks, so he changed them.'

'Something like that,' said Mr Darwin vaguely, still gazing at the far hills. 'Perhaps, possibly. Who knows? Some change their beaks, some their tails. Some even change colour to blend with their backgrounds. It's all very odd.'

Elizabeth was confused by this strange man, one moment all vitality and eager curiosity, the next lapsing into long silences. At that moment he sat staring at the ground between his feet. He seemed to have forgotten that they were there.

William also, on his other side, appeared lost in thought. I'd like that,' he said finally, turning his impish grin toward Mr Darwin.

'What?'

'To change colour. If I was a bird, I could turn blue to match the sky.' He thought for a moment. 'Why aren't all birds blue then? And why are we pink? That doesn't go with anything.'

Mr Darwin laughed. 'I don't think it's quite that simple,' he said, then sighed. 'No, it's not that simple. Why is it not that simple?' He returned to staring at his feet. He looked so anxious and alone. Elizabeth felt a twinge of guilt that she was not a better companion. But what an absurd thing to look so worried about, the shape of a bird's beak!

'Mr Darwin, it doesn't really matter, truly it doesn't,' she said on impulse, then felt silly.

He looked up and smiled wanly. 'It does to me,' he said.

They were interrupted by the sound of the garden gate being opened and shut. They turned to see Mr Williams coming along the path.

'Meeting over,' he announced, holding up a large bag. 'I'm off to the market. I thought you might like to come. We hold it once a week to trade with the local Maoris.'

Mr Darwin leapt to his feet. 'That sounds interesting. What do you trade?'

'There's little value in money here, it's all done by barter.'

Mr Darwin turned apologetically to the children. 'Please excuse me if I go with Mr Williams. I'm keen to see this barter,' he explained.

'Oh no! They come too, we couldn't do it without them,' said Mr Williams.

'How's that?'

'They are our interpreters; we adults have learnt Maori but the children grew up with it. They are far quicker and understand it better.' He turned to the children. 'You don't mind coming, do you? The others all seem to be away collecting plants for Mr Darwin.'

Elizabeth and William nodded in agreement and followed the men out of the garden, to where the market was held, in the open space between the house and the church.

Mrs Davis, the farm manager's wife, was there already and looked relieved when she saw the children.

'I see you have two helpers; can I borrow one?' she asked. 'I'm having a terrible time.'

William was dispatched to help her.

The men ambled around the square, looking at the goods neatly laid out on flax mats. Elizabeth followed them. Mr Williams made a few purchases, gaining corn and a couple of flax baskets in exchange for clothing and tobacco which seemed to be in demand.

One man asked for vegetable seeds and Mr Williams promised to get him some.

'They prefer to buy them from us,' he explained, 'after some rascally sailor sold them dock seeds, saying they were tobacco seeds. They are still trying to get rid of the docks.'

'That's understandable then, but is tobacco any use to them either? You seem to do a lot of trade with that.'

'Also introduced by the sailors, but it seems harmless if somewhat addictive.'

As if he had heard the conversation, an old man suddenly accosted Mr Williams. He held up a flax basket.

'Kumara,' he announced. He held out his other hand, palm up. 'Tobacco?'

'Aie,' answered Mr Williams, burrowing into his bag and producing some tobacco. 'Ask him if he would like some soap, too. He looks as though he needs it.'

'*E patai ana Wiremu pena e hiahia hopi ana koe?*' asked Elizabeth, relaying the enquiry.

'*Hopi?*' queried the old man, '*He aha tena, hena homai kia kite ahau.*'

'He would like to see it,' she explained

Mr Williams reached into his bag and produced some soap.

'*Aue tena mea!*' said the man with a look of disgust on his face. '*Homai e koe tetahi i tera o haere nga mai. Tino kino te haware o taku mangai. Ka ruaki ahau. Hore ata he mea morikarika.*'

'He says he got some last time and it is terrible.'

'Why is that?'

Elizabeth giggled. 'He says it doesn't taste too good.'

Both the men laughed, and the look of anger on the man's face was plain to see.

'*He mahi kino te whaka hawea ite kaumatua, kanui taku rikarika.*'

Elizabeth could see that his dignity was offended and roughly translated his words to the two men. 'He says it is not a good thing to make fun of an old man.'

She attempted to make amends. *'Kanui taku pouri hore kau koe I mohio tika e hara te hopi mo te kai. E ngari hei horoi kakahu, me te tinana kia pai te ma.'*

'What are you saying to him, Elizabeth?'

'I am just telling him not to eat it, that it's for washing. I think he was upset that you laughed at him.

The man, however, was not appeased. *'Ka haere ahau kit e koukou i te awa me aku kakahu, kia ma ai ahau, me aku kakahu.'*

'He says he is clean, he washes in the river.'

Elizabeth could see that more placating was necessary. *'Te pai ote hanga oto hāte, e ngari e paru ana te hanga,'* she said.

'He hāte tawhito ke tenei,' he thundered.

Elizabeth saw an opportunity. *'Ma te hopi ka hou ano te hanga oto hāte,'* she pronounced. The old man laughed and turned away.

'Elizabeth, would you please tell us what you are chattering about?'

'I'm just telling him that soap would make his shirt look like new again.'

'That's hardly truthful, Elizabeth. Can't you see that it is an old one.'

'That's just what he said!' claimed Elizabeth with a grin.

Mr Williams picked up his bag and started to move on but William suddenly rushed up to Elizabeth and grabbed her by the skirt.

'Come over here,' he urged. 'I can see the dray coming from Kerikeri, and Mrs Davis saw it too. We think Mama's on it.'

Elizabeth looked where William was pointing. 'It looks like it,' she agreed. 'It might be Papa, coming to collect us.'

They watched intently as the horse and dray came crawling up the hill. It disappeared behind patches of bush and folds of land but reappeared, each time a little larger and a little more distinct.

'It is, that's our horse,' said William.

'And Papa. But who's with him? There are two, no, three other people. Do you think it could be Mama?' said Elizabeth.

'Come on, let's go and see,' said William, rushing off down the path towards the house.

Elizabeth took a few steps along the path then stopped and turned back. Mr Darwin was standing talking to Mr Williams. She felt she should apologize for leaving but nothing else seemed to matter at the moment except that her mother might be well again. Suddenly she had the sense that there was some hope in the world and that, given time, most things do come right, and most griefs are overcome. It was fleeting and hard to explain in words. She decided to carry on and apologize later.

CHAPTER 16

Elizabeth limped around the corner of the Clarkes' house to find the dray drawn up at the front door. William had already scrambled up beside his mother to hug her.

Two men descended from the back. Elizabeth recognised one as Mr Nisbet but the second, younger one was unfamiliar, until he turned towards her. He grinned. 'Lizzie!'

She hesitated. 'Not Henry?'

'Who else?' He spread his hands.

'Oh! How you've grown.'

'For goodness' sake, Lizzie, what a greeting. You sound like an aged aunt. Of course I've grown in two years. You don't look to have shrunk, either.'

'Henry, it's really you!' She took a couple of hops forward and threw her arms round him, letting her crutches fall to the ground. 'When did you come? Why didn't you let us know? Why are you home so soon?'

'Steady on; I arrived yesterday. Aunt Ann wrote, but the boat I was on caught up to the one she sent the letter on. So we both arrived together, practically.' He bent and retrieved her crutches.

Elizabeth was completely overcome. It was all more than she had hoped for. Henry was back. Her mother, pale, and looking calmer than the last time she had seen her, now descended from the dray. Though she lacked her former confident air, Elizabeth could see that she had improved considerably. The tears welled up in her eyes as she hopped forward to greet her. Without saying a word, her mother hugged her tight and, feeling the strength and firmness of her touch, Elizabeth knew that she was getting better.

Her mother kept hold of her hand as Elizabeth lead her into the house. They were met by Mrs Clarke coming out to see the new arrivals, closely followed by Hopkins.

'Charlotte,' she clasped her friend's other hand, 'how wonderful to see you looking so much better. Come, sit down; you too, Elizabeth. I'll go and make a pot of tea. James, the men have gone to the market following a committee meeting. They should be back any moment.'

To Elizabeth, drying her tears, it seemed as though the world was pulling itself together from a scattering of fragments. Helping to endorse this feeling, people began to converge. Mrs Davis and Mr Williams, having seen the arrivals, came from the direction of the market. Several children appeared in the doorway carrying bunches of leaves. They were told to await Mr Darwin on the verandah.

Hopkins came and attached himself to Elizabeth's skirt, looking at her with dog-like devotion. She lifted him onto her knee. Mr Williams came across to the Kemps.

'James, Charlotte, the best of news for you. The committee has just decided. You are not to go!'

'Go? Where?' asked Mr Kemp.

'Anywhere!' said Mr Williams, 'You are to stay at Kerikeri.'

'Then you will let us keep the house. I'm pleased about that.'

'No, James, don't you understand? We have not accepted your resignation. You are to carry on at Kerikeri as before — well, almost.'

'You mean …' A shadow of disbelief crossed Mr Kemp's face. 'I can continue with my work?'

'Yes, aren't you pleased?' said Mr Williams. 'But there will have to be some changes. Mr Shepherd will be going to Whangaroa. And you will have to work alone. But we will talk about it later. Lovely to see you, Charlotte. It's good that you are looking so well.'

More and more people seemed to congregate in the house, children and adults. Greetings were called, cheeks were kissed, everybody talked. Mrs Clarke organised. She soon had everyone sorted into groups for lunch. Mr Williams and Mr Darwin were placed in the first relay, so that they could inspect the kauri trees before the Christmas service.

'And not too late back,' she instructed. 'The Paihia and Kerikeri people have to get home before dark. William, put into water the plants Mr Darwin wishes to keep, and Martha, sweep the leaves away.'

To Elizabeth, sitting in the corner with Hopkins on her knee, she nodded and said, 'That's right, dear,' as she swept past.

Elizabeth caught her mother's eye across the room. They both smiled. She looked about and felt at peace. Hopkins lay back and sucked his thumb. Her father and Mr Davis stood before the window, discussing something. The sun threw a fringe of light about their heads. She could tell, by the way her father kept looking at his fingers, that he was asking for something. He always did that, as though the examination of his hands was a way of being non-committal about his request. She noticed James hovering near, as though anxious about the outcome. Yes, it was definitely about James. Mr Davis grasped him by the shoulder and drew him closer. She could not hear a word they were saying, but she could see from the look of happiness on James' face, and the benign expressions of the two men, that something had been agreed upon.

Good, James was settled. Her mother was well. Henry was back. Her father looked happier than he had for months and she was happy, too! Elizabeth gave Hopkins a squeeze. He gurgled, thumb in mouth, and dribbled down his chin.

Mrs Clarke paused as she passed and took out her hand-kerchief. 'Oh, Hopkins,' she said, removing his thumb and wiping it dry. 'I'll take him for lunch now, Lizzie. Come and have some yourself.' Elizabeth followed her through to the kitchen.

Mr Nisbet appeared to be the only person there. He was finishing his lunch. Elizabeth sat beside him.

'Hello, lassie,' he said. 'Did you know I'm going?'

'Going? Where?'

'I've finished at Kerikeri now. I've done my jobs for the mission. I'm going back to Horeke where I was before. Some of my friends have started a mill there.'

'A flour mill?'

'No lass, a timber mill. There'll be a demand for timber soon. There's a few settlers starting to come. And boats are always needing timber, for repairs and spars and the like.'

'I'm sorry you're going.'

'Well, so am I, in a way. We've had some good times and some bad, but we muddled through, didn't we?'

'Yes.'

'Well, that's how it is — some goes well and some not so well. People come, and people go.'

'Did you finish my splint?' asked Elizabeth.

'Yes, it's there waiting for you. Your father and I finished it. It's lighter, much lighter, with a neat little shoe on it to put your foot in.'

'Thank you, it's very kind of you to go to all that bother for me.'

Mr Nisbet stood up and pushed his chair back. 'Aye, bless you. Well, I must be off. It's a long way to Horeke before dark. ''Bye, lass!' He patted her head.

''Bye,' said Elizabeth as she watched him walk to the door. 'I'll keep on muddling,' she called after him.

'Not much else we can do.' He smiled, and was gone.

After lunch they all squeezed into the chapel for a short Christmas service, taken by Reverend Williams. The church was decked in white for the festival. Bowls of white flowers stood by the altar. The building was filled with the scent of roses and lilies from the garden. The Kemps sat together, squashed up on the front bench. Their father sat at the end, as he had to read the first lesson. Elizabeth was so elated she found it hard to concentrate on anything, but she caught the last few words of her father's reading: '"… and the light shineth in darkness, and the darkness comprehendeth it not."'

The insistence of the well-known phrase brought to mind the months of darkness that had just passed, and the dark scudding clouds of night that had distorted her mother's mind. But there had been light, too. The light of the boat bringing her father up the river, and the light of the fire that night, as he comforted her. She recalled, farther back, the darkness and the wet grass by the hen-house on the night that Sam died; and the deep thunderous sky as she and the Clarkes rode up to Waimate, then the bright new potato shoots growing up through the black ground. New life growing from the darkness.

By the time she directed her mind back to the service, it was nearly over and she was just in time to join in the last hymn, 'Hark the Herald Angels Sing' before the congregation was dismissed. They filed out and stood chatting, and calling, 'Happy Christmas,' as they parted.

Mr Kemp soon had the horse harnessed to the dray again and the Kerikeri people gathered around. He looked in alarm at all the children. Fifteen of them: a mixture of Edmonds, Kemps and Shepherds. 'I'm sorry, some of you will have to walk. Consider the poor old horse.'

There were groans of dismay and laughter, but the bigger children set off down the track.

Mrs Kemp, Elizabeth and the smallest children clambered aboard. Even then there were six children and Mr Kemp warned them that on the uphill stretch, they too would have to get out and walk.

On the downward run to the Waitangi river they soon overtook the walkers but, once over the bridge, the children had to dismount for the slow, uphill trudge. Elizabeth got off too, to encourage the little ones. They soon heard the cheery shouts of the boys as they came striding up behind them. Two of the bigger boys picked up Sarah and little Henry Edmonds and carried them to the summit. Having seen them aboard the dray again, they waved goodbye. And, with a derisive shout of, 'We'll be home before you!' they jogged ahead.

Mr Kemp gave the horse a rest as the other children caught up and clambered aboard.

The sun was just starting to disappear behind the western horizon as they crested the hill. The Bay of Islands lay ahead, the islands seeming to float like ships between sea and sky as the dusk deepened. Looking back, they could see the faint lights of Waimate across the valley. Above, the moon was a glowing hemisphere. A few stars shone. The horse knew the way home and plodded forward.

William sat, crouched at Elizabeth's feet, his head tilted back against her knee. 'If I were a night bird,' he murmured, 'I'd be dark blue. And I'd get darker and darker, until it was night.'

The dray rumbled on, occasionally jolting over a stone or rut. Up on the front seat, Sarah dropped off to sleep. Her mother put a protective arm around her and turned back to Elizabeth.

'Is William asleep?' she whispered.

'No, I'm not,' said William. 'I'm looking at the sky.'

Mrs Kemp looked up. 'It's a perfect night,' she said.

'If I were God, and I lived in the sky, I would make myself dark, dark blue and sprinkle myself with shiny stars.'

'Then nobody would know whether you were there or not,' said Elizabeth.

The dray jerked down the last steep hill towards their house.

The boys must have got there first. The lights shone from the kitchen.

They were all home again, together.

POSTSCRIPT

Shortly after the period written about in this book, the staff at the mission were reduced to one family — the Kemps. They continued with their work, teaching and looking after the trading store. It was not until 1860 that they were able to buy the house.

As the children grew up they were able to take over and farm their share of the 'children's land'. Elizabeth continued teaching at the girls' and women's school that her mother had set up. With her fluency in both languages Elizabeth was able to teach English to many of the Maori girls.

Several years later, as soon as Hopkins Clarke reached the age of twenty-one, he married Elizabeth despite their age difference. They seem to have lived a long and happy life with their two children, farming their share of the family land near Kerikeri.

The Kemps' house, which is pictured on the cover of this book, was lived in by four more generations of the family until Ernest Kemp gave it to the nation in 1976.

It is now maintained by the Historic Places Trust and can be visited by the public. The stone store building exchanged hands several times until it too, was acquired by the trust.

Though they are often criticised, I think the missionaries were very brave people to leave their homes and families in England, in many cases never to see them again, and travel to the opposite side of the world to help people who lived very differently.

The children of missionaries, however, were born in New Zealand and they knew little else. This is my imagined version of their lives, but based on as many facts and true incidents as I have been able to discover.

Brenda Delamain
24th January, 2006